The
Frencn
for
Christmas

The
French
for
Christmas

FIONA VALPY

Bookouture

Published by Bookouture

An imprint of StoryFire Ltd.
23 Sussex Road, Ickenham, UB10 8PN
United Kingdom

www.bookouture.com

ISBN: 978-1-909490-64-2
eBook ISBN: 978-1-909490-63-5

For Friends and Family,
who make Christmas merry and bright.

Acknowledgements

Whilst the setting for this book is very close to home, every character and incident is purely fictitious: any resemblances to real people or real places—other than those that you can find named on a map—are purely coincidental. I owe a debt of gratitude to many lovely people who have inspired aspects of the story though...

A huge thank you to Beth Nielsen Chapman, singer/songwriter extraordinaire, for her kind permission to include the words from 'Every December Sky' here. If you haven't discovered her songs already then I would urge you to check out her website for more details of her wonderful work: http://bethnielsenchapman.com/

Heartfelt thanks to Paul Fenton for sparing so much of his precious time to tell me about the problems and challenges anaesthetists face when working in the developing world. Having worked in Africa, and having developed the Universal Anaesthetic Machine which is now being distributed worldwide by Gradian Health Systems, Paul provided key inspiration for this story. For more informa-

tion about Gradian's work and the Universal Anaesthetic Machine, please visit http://www.gradianhealth.org

Thank you to my American family—the Thompsons (John and Carol, Rupert, Laura and Maya), the Hochmans (Juliet, Steve, Nate and Thomas), and the Somols (Jessica, Mark, Charlotte and Emma)—for those wonderfully memorable holidays on golden pond in both summer and winter. And special thanks to Juliet Thompson Hochman for being my American language consultant.

As ever, merci beaucoup to the team at Bookouture for all their help and support: Oliver Rhodes, Emily Ruston, Claire Bord, Kim Nash, Lorella Belli and Debbie Brunettin.

And love and thanks to my friends and family—especially Rupert, James and Alastair—who have supported and encouraged me in my writing, and who make Christmas Christmas.

Every December Sky

Every December sky
Must lose its faith in leaves
And dream of the spring inside the trees.
How heavy the empty heart,
How light the heart that's full
Sometimes I have to trust what I can't know,
Sometimes I have to trust what I can't know.

Beth Nielsen Chapman

Chapter 1
Deck the Halls

Deck the halls with boughs of holly,
Fa la la la la, la la la la.
'Tis the season to be jolly,
Fa la la la la, la la la la.

We're sitting at Rose's kitchen table in the aftermath of the final book club meeting of the year, the last Friday in November. The others have all left, making their way home to their families, looking forward to their busy weekends. But I'm lingering in the bright warmth of Rose's kitchen, pretending to make myself useful collecting up glasses and plates, reluctant to go back and push open the door to my own darkened house, knowing that its emptiness will ring loud in my ears. Avoiding the sad silence of the rooms where my grief lives behind their shut doors, decomposing quietly until it loses enough of its radioactive power to be handled safely. How many half-lives will that be, I wonder?

Rose's husband, Max, pokes his head round the doorway. 'Is it safe to come out yet?' He'd been banished to his study for the evening, the book club being a girls-only affair, and now he's come to claim his reward from the dishes of leftovers that clutter the kitchen table. He gives me a hug. 'How's my favourite Yankee redhead? And is there any of your quiche left, Evie? Oh, good,' he sighs, taking a bite. 'Delicious as ever.'

'I know,' Rose nods, breaking off the corner of the last slice left in the dish and savouring the rich mix of Comté cheese and smoked bacon. 'You've given me the recipe, but it never tastes as good when I make it. Must be your French-Irish-American *je ne sais quoi*.' She raises her glass with a flourish. '*Santé*! Or should that be *Slainte*?'

She pours some more wine into my glass and then tips the dregs into her own, raising it to the light so that it gleams with a soft ruby glow. Her expression is thoughtful. 'When are you going to think about getting back in the saddle again, Evie? Your talent's going to waste, you know. There must be restaurants out there that would snap you up. Or maybe you could try your hand at writing a few articles for one of the cookery magazines?'

'Don't push her, Rose.' Max reaches over to pat my arm. 'All in good time, after the year she's had.'

I smile at him, thankful for his kindness. By now, most people have stopped being kind, or openly so at least. They've moved on with their own lives, leaving me stuck back here at the point where mine stopped. I feel like I'm watching them all disappearing off over the horizon without a backward glance as I stand forlornly, mired here in the quicksand of my grief, weighted down by my anger.

Not waving, but drowning.

'I've promised myself I'll get back onto it in the New Year. There's no point now with December just round the corner. I'll get through Christmas and then see.' And, while I'm trying to keep my tone light and even, I confess I'm terrified at the prospect: I don't know yet whether I'm going to stay on in London or move back to Boston. Such big decisions require energy and I'm fresh out of that right now. I hope I sound more upbeat than I feel, but Rose fixes me with her gimlet gaze, the one that she uses to such good effect, to see through the surface veneer of fake cheerfulness to the truth underneath.

'Ah, yes, and speaking of Christmas, what are your plans? Max and I would be delighted if you would come and spend the day with us. I promise not to make you cook a thing.'

Max looks a little crestfallen. 'Or, well, maybe just one of your pies if you felt like it?' he suggests. 'I've never really liked Christmas pudding and your blueberry one is my absolute favourite. Or what's that upside-down apple thing with the caramel?'

'*Tarte Tatin*?'

'That's the one. Delicious!'

'Back off, Max,' Rose warns with a protective snarl. 'She doesn't have to cook anything.'

I sigh, reluctant to think about Christmas at all. All those memories of last year, coming home from the hospital on Christmas Eve to a houseful of shattered dreams; Will unable to bring himself to look at the shadows of pain and grief etched onto my face as he set my overnight case down carefully on the bed, treading cautiously, as if we might both break into a thousand pieces at any sudden move. He'd closed the door softly behind him and left me to unpack. I was still sitting there, the case unopened beside me, when he came back to check on me an hour later.

I wasn't angry with him then, only stunned and shocked with grief.

The anger came later.

'That's really kind. I just don't know... I'm still wondering whether I shouldn't go back to the States. Though it feels kind of cowardly to run away.'

In fact the real reason I'm even thinking twice about it is because I can't face my mother's determined cheerfulness, her efforts to involve me in the childbirth charity she's now fundraising for, which is typical of her way of coping; she's always been a doer, strong enough to face anything head-on and find a way to move forward. She won't be able to understand why I can't do the same.

That, and the fact that my sister Tess is seven months pregnant: the exact same stage I was at Christmas last year. None of us is saying it, but I know they're holding their breath, praying that her baby will make it through, even though there's no earthly reason why it shouldn't.

But then there was no earthly reason why my baby's heart stopped beating. Just one of those things, they said...

I try to summon a smile for Rose and Max and their invitation. 'I don't know; it's just that Will's face is going to be everywhere here with this new TV series. Last week I had to do a body-swerve in the supermarket when I came face-to-face with a copy of the *Radio Times*.'

The magazine trumpeted "Will Brooke's Delicious December Dining", his face beaming out at me from the front cover. Flustered by a surge of conflicting emotions, I'd steered my trolley into a festive stack (already!) of tins of Danish butter cookies, sending them clattering across the floor. I still feel guilty about leaving them there, their fragile contents no doubt reduced to piles of crumbs. I'd stumbled out of the shop and sat shaking in my car, my hands fumbling as I tried to fit the key into the ignition.

Rose takes my hand, her expression one of tender concern. Uh-oh, something's up: she's not usually the sentimental type. I brace myself.

'Evie, I don't know if you've seen this?' She pulls a gossip magazine out from under a pile of glossier ones. I shake my head. 'I thought not. Well, I think you do need to see it before anyone else mentions it.' She turns to a two-page spread, where Will's face beams out at me again. "Will Power!" shouts the headline. "Celebrity chef Will Brooke talks about his tragic loss and new beginnings as he launches his series of festive cookery programmes." Rose sits back, allowing me time to scan the article and digest what's on the page. It's mostly pictures of him in his apron, wielding a kitchen knife and presenting a steaming pot pie—my grandmother's recipe, I note, with my cranberry glaze which, though I do say so myself, looks very attractive. But the final picture is a less posed one, a fuzzy shot of him snapped in the street with his arm around the shoulder of a pretty blonde. "Something's cooking: we can reveal Will's mystery girl is Stephanie Wallis, an assistant on the new show."

My stomach knots as I take in the photo and the chatty text beneath it. And then I read, "Brave Will is trying to put the tragedy of losing the baby behind him and focus on his future. As he so rightly says, the show must go on!"

I fold the magazine shut, feeling nauseous, and place it very carefully on the table in front of me. Rose and Max are sitting on either side, watching me intently, and Rose puts a hand on my arm again. Her touch brings me to. I turn to look at her, trying to summon a scornful smile at this ridiculous article in this trashy magazine. But my face won't behave the way I want it to. Of its own accord, it crumples and collapses. And Rose pulls me to her as I begin to sob uncontrollably. 'At last,' she says, matter-of-factly. 'I was wondering if you were *ever* going to cry.'

It's true, it's the first time I've cried in a long, long while; I thought I'd gotten pretty good at covering my true feelings, but this has caught me unawares. So it takes me a bit of time to regain control and be able to take the Kleenex Max is offering me and blow my nose. I look at Rose's face and see that she, too, has tears in her eyes.

She knows how I feel because she was there, through the whole terrible ordeal. This must be conjuring up painful memories for her as well. She was the one who came to the hospital when I called her because Will was up in Manchester and too busy with the filming of an episode of *On Your Marks, Get Set, Cook!* which, he was hoping, would lead to bigger and better things. Admittedly it was my own fault too. I told him not to rush back. After all, by then there was nothing he could do; there was no heartbeat; the baby was gone. And the hospital said they'd leave it for a day or two before they induced my labour. I should just go home and take a few days to let it sink in; there was no rush. So, when I told him this, Will said, 'Okay, if you're absolutely sure, Evie. I'll be home tomorrow night anyway. And if you've got Rose there with you for the time being...' How was either of us to know the contractions would start spontaneously that night, too late for him to get a train or hire a car? So that, by the time he arrived at the hospital, all that was left for him to do was to hold our child, just that once, and then bring me home. Back to a house that felt as empty and sad as I did myself.

'Sorry, Evie,' Rose says.

'That's okay. You had to show me the article. Better that I know what's out there. But, you know, I'm just not sure I can do it.' I start to cry again, blotting my eyes with the soggy paper. 'I have to get away. I can't stay here with all this,' I wave a hand at the magazine, 'but I can't go home to America either. I want to cancel Christmas and crawl away into a cave somewhere where I can be on my own. I just can't face the fun and the glitz and the Delicious Dining and the Festive Feasts. You're so kind to invite me to join you, but it'd ruin it for all of you, tiptoeing around me in case something sets me off again. I have to get away. But there's nowhere for me to go.' My voice shakes with fear and wretchedness, and fury at Will and his mystery girl, and—okay, okay, I admit it—self-pity.

Rose and Max exchange a glance and he nods. 'We thought that might be the case.' Rose pats my hand again. 'So we've come up with a Plan B. Why don't you go and spend Christmas in the house in France? You can take yourself off there for some peace and some space and have a complete break. It's not so far to go that you'll be stuck if you change your mind and want to come back to London and spend Christmas with us after all, but you'll be able to escape the media circus there. And you know how you love French cuisine. Who knows, it might do you good to get back to your roots. Maybe you could even start researching an article or two.'

I shake my head. I've definitely lost my cooking mojo and, right now, the last thing I want to think about is facing up to the collapse of my career, let alone the rest of my life.

Max pats my other hand. 'You don't have to force yourself to do anything, Evie. Just take some time out. Plonk yourself down there with a few bottles of the local wine and perhaps an occasional quiche.' Max reaches out his hand for the remainder of the last slice and raises it in a jaunty salute, 'Use it as a time to recharge your batteries. Things might look clearer from a distance. And at the very least you'll be spared the shopping frenzy and the continuous tacky Christmas music, and the conspicuous consumption and the completely crap weather that we'll be bombarded with here. In fact, come to think of it, it sounds quite tempting. Perhaps I'll come and join you.' The pastry crust crumbles as he sinks his teeth into it, scattering golden crumbs down his shirt front.

'Over my dead body, Max Morgan!' retorts Rose. 'I know you'd far rather be in France with your favourite American than back here in grey London with your stressed-out harridan of a wife and your children arguing with you about which film to watch on the telly, but you're staying here.'

'Ah, well, since you put it like that... And a very merry Christmas to you too, my darling!' Max kisses her fondly on the top of her head as he carries the now empty quiche dish over to the sink.

I sit and think, Rose's offer sinking in slowly. It does sound tempting. And escaping would be a neat solution to my woes. I glance at the gossip magazine again. In fact... 'How soon could I go?'

Rose follows my gaze and then beams at me. 'Why, as soon as you like! The house is sitting empty; it's yours for as long as you want it.'

I wipe the mascara from under my eyes and blow my nose again. 'Could I maybe go next week? Plan on spending the whole of December there?'

'Of course you can my darling... and with not a Festive Feast in sight!'

I manage to summon a watery grin and pick up the magazine again. 'Oh, well, at least he gives me a mention. I read aloud: "Will and his ex-wife opened the highly successful Brooke's Bistro five years ago but sold the business last year as Will's career took off. 'My wife, Evie, was the wind beneath my wings,' explains Will, 'but sadly we've grown apart.'" I sigh, hoping for sympathy. I should have known better.

Rose guffaws. 'And just when did the wind beneath his wings turn into the doormat beneath his feet, might I ask? Honestly, Evie, you were always the true talent in the partnership and Will knows that. I give him a year. He'll soon realise how much he needs you and your recipes once the honeymoon period wears off. And by that time I hope you'll have realised it yourself and be back in the kitchen, getting the recognition you deserve in your own right. And then he'll be sorry.' Her expression softens as I wipe another tear away. 'Come on love, you just need a bit more time, that's all. Life happens, you know? Of course you're battered and bruised right now, who wouldn't be? But I promise you, you will come out the other side of this and be stronger than before. I'm so glad you're going to France. It'll be the perfect break, a chance to get some perspective on what you want to do next.'

I nod. 'You're right. And you know what? Life sure as hell happens, but at least this year I can make sure

Christmas won't. Not for me at least. And for that I am truly grateful to you both.'

'You sure you'll be okay?' Rose asks as she stands in the doorway to see me out. She hugs me. 'Come straight back if you don't want to be in the house alone.'

'I'm fine. Got a busy weekend ahead of me. I'm off to France, dontcha know, and I've got some serious packing to do. Anyway, don't worry; if I find myself at loose ends there's always *The Playbook*!'

Rose and I are agreed that *'The Silver Linings Playbook'* is our very favourite movie of all time. Currently at least: we reserve the right to replace it at some future point, just as it replaced *'Dirty Dancing'* (Rose's long-standing choice) and *'It's Complicated'* (mine, because of the scene with the *croque-monsieurs* as well as the one with Alec Baldwin and the webcam). But, for the time being, The Playbook, as we like to refer to it, is our favourite for the following three reasons:

1. Bradley Cooper is gorgeous.
2. The two main characters have both been made crazy by grief and anger and, for them as for me, this craziness feels more normal and more rational than the so-called sanity of everyone else in the world.
3. Bradley Cooper is gorgeous.

I suspect in Rose's case only reasons (1) and (3) apply.

A late-fall fog hangs in the air as I walk back through the lamplit streets, my heels tapping on the London sidewalk with new purpose. Now, instead of dreading the blankness of the weekend that stretches before me, I'm looking forward to it. I have work to do: I need to book my crossing, do my packing, tidy the house. Plan my escape back to my beloved France. My heart lifts as I realise I can even swing by Paris on the way down. Am I ready for that walk down memory lane, I ask myself? And, to my surprise, I think maybe I am. I can't wait to step back to a time before sadness and fear, when life was there for the taking.

It was thanks to my darling grandmother, *Mamie* Lucie, and her bequest to me of the notebook full of recipes and enough money for a ticket across the Atlantic, that the world suddenly opened up before me and became, as the saying goes, my *huître*. Memories flood back to me as I walk home through the damp streets: my first day at the cookery school, with its bright, spotlessly clean counters and sets of gleaming utensils at each station, the air smelling faintly—like the best restaurants do—of butter and the subtle undertones of dill and white wine from the fish dish that the students had been cooking that morning; an evening in a bar with my fellow students from the four corners of the world, an exciting mix of cultures, complexions, accents, all of us laughing as English Will did his impersonation of the chef, Monsieur Charles, tasting the bouillon and declaring it an 'abomination'. We nicknamed him 'Prince William' because he did bear a passing resemblance to the second in line to the British throne with his blond good looks and polished manners. He had charisma, even then, and was always the star of the show.

And then there are those other, more private memories: Will's eyes meeting mine above the rim of my wineglass, something clicking into place, a connection, a certainty; lying together, tangled in the sheets, in my tiny one-room apartment high up amongst the Parisian rooftops; Will standing on the bed to push open the roof light, craning his head and saying, 'Hey! You can even see the Eiffel Tower from here!' then holding me steady as I joined him on tiptoes on the shifting, lumpy mattress and we gazed out across a petrified forest of redundant chimney pots and TV antennas to where the lights of Paris's most iconic landmark twinkled and winked at us. As if it was sharing in our joy and our exhilaration at having found each other in the city of love.

I reach the high street, my stream of thoughts interrupted by the necessity of crossing the busy stream of London traffic. On the other side I hesitate, choosing which route to take back to the house. Recently I've been taking the longer way round, sticking to the main streets and avoiding the cut-through where the bistro used to be. But tonight, in my newfound glow of positivity, I decide to be brave and so I turn the toes of my boots in the direction of the antique shops and quirkier boutiques.

'*Fabio's Ristorante Italiano*' the new sign reads, its red neon infusing the November fog with a garish chemical glow. 'Book your Christmas lunch now!' is scrawled on a chalkboard outside. 'Special menu!' I walk on, picking up the pace as I try not to remember how it used to be when the sign read 'Brooke's Bistro' in old-gold lettering. I would set each table with soft linens and a little vase of fresh flowers, and write the daily menu of dishes made from whatever produce was fresh and in season on that same chalkboard.

I make it past, my heart rate quickening a bit, I note, but nothing too much more overwhelming than that. Progress. A small triumph.

But my sense of achievement falters and then sputters out like a candle drowning in its own wax as

I reach my front door and grope in the bottom of my purse for the keys.

'*France!*' I whisper to myself. '*Focus on that. Nothing else.*'

I push the door open, stepping into the hushed warmth of the hallway and the silent sadness of this space that should have been filled with my husband's welcoming arms and the gurgling smiles of our baby daughter.

Should-a, would-a, could-a. All those might-have-beens. Some of the emptiest words there are.

I wipe my feet on the doormat before easing off my boots, and as I do, Rose's comment comes back to me. '*And just when did the wind beneath his wings become the doormat beneath his feet?*' A throwaway remark, but one that stings a little I have to admit. The truth hurts, as they say.

I set my boots neatly side by side beneath the coat hooks. As I straighten up, I can't help brushing my fingers over the faded fabric of an old jacket of Will's that he's left behind, the elbows rubbed shiny with wear, un-needed in his newer, more glamorous life. Was it my fault he left? Was it my anger that drove him away? Or was it his own guilt?

The bistro had been a true partnership, each of us bringing our own particular skills to the business. I supplied the ideas for menus and he had the strength and the unflagging energy that the gruelling daily routine in the kitchen demanded. At first we worked side by side, Will as head chef while I did the baking, preparing our trademark home-made breads and pastries, and ran the front of house. The most popular dish on the lunch menu was always my wheaten soda bread (in homage to my Irish roots), spread thick with unsalted French butter and served with the soup of the day: true comfort food and the best and simplest kind of fusion *cuisine*.

Then, when I fell pregnant—a miracle, so soon after we decided to start trying, because the business was on solid foundations, its popularity starting to soar—I began to struggle to keep up with the schedule. I was exhausted, battling with the nausea as the morning sickness hit me hard. 'Never mind,' Will had reassured me. 'You rest. We can afford the extra staff to cover your areas. Just do the lunchtime shifts, if you're up to it.'

I thought I'd get my energy back after the first trimester. After all, that's how it's supposed to be, isn't it? Women glowing with pregnancy, radiating an abundance of serene energy as they morph into motherhood? Only not in my case. The nausea never really abated, which meant that being around food became a torture instead of the joy it used to be. First I went off coffee—even the smell of it made my stomach heave; the sight of a glass of wine brought acid surging into my throat; the sight of Will filleting mackerel made me gag; and the thought of whipping a bowl of cream had my insides lurching like a butter-churn. All of which is a bit of a handicap when you work in a restaurant.

I couldn't bow out completely though. I cared too passionately about the bistro (my other baby!) so I'd drag myself in to help set up for lunch and dinner and chalk the *plat du jour* on the board, swallowing hard. Some days, when I felt a little stronger, I'd get back into the kitchen, adding my trademark touches to certain dishes, suggesting recipes to Will depending on what fresh produce we had that day. And back home I'd experiment with new recipes, digging into *Mamie* Lucie's tattered notebook and deciphering her spidery handwriting, with frequent consultations of my French dictionary whenever I came across an ingredient or an instruction that I wasn't sure of. Trying to contribute to the bistro's menus as best I could.

And then came the day when, as I was arranging the vase of flowers for the front desk (one of the few chores that I still positively enjoyed), I felt that first tiny movement inside of me. Not the churning of my gut, but something else, deep inside my belly. A flutter, as delicate and persistent as the wings of a butterfly against a windowpane: my baby moving, kicking her tiny heels against the walls that confined her. I froze. Then placed my hand over the spot, willing her to do it again. And she did. As if she heard me ask the question, and she kicked back in reply.

And in that moment my heart was locked to hers with a strength so fierce that it took my breath away.

I spoke to her constantly from then on. I'd tell her about the day's menu as I wrote it out and she'd drum her heels approvingly; I'd breathe deep the scent of the white trumpet-like lilies on the front desk as I passed, hoping their perfume would infuse my bloodstream so that she would be surrounded by it too; and I'd gently caress my ballooning belly, calling to Will to come and feel the butterfly movements as our daughter stretched and flexed and reached out to us from the dark warmth of her cocoon.

For me, though, the radiant stage never materialised. My back ached, and I grew even more exhausted as the months rolled slowly by. I longed for the day when our baby would be born, finally separate from me so that I could try to regain some kind of balance in my life, freed at last from the dense fog of sick exhaustion that smothered me throughout my pregnancy. And I'll admit, I feel overwhelmed with guilt now, remembering this. I'd give anything to have her still moving in my belly. Unconsciously, I put a hand on the flat front of my jeans, my stomach concave between the sharply jutting hipbones. Empty. Realising, I jerk my hand away, as though from the scalding rim of a hot pan.

The silence in the house closes in around me like a soft blanket.

I prefer being alone these days. Because, strictly between you and me, ever since last Christmas Eve I've been living two lives. One involves silence and distance and pain and loss. It's a lonely life, where my husband has left me, unable to bear the weight of my grief on top of his own; unable to soothe my anger and his guilt; unable to accept that I can't move on when he can.

It's reality.

My second life, which runs on a parallel track, is an imaginary one, and I escape into it whenever I can. Because it's filled with light and noise and love. In it, Will is still here and our beautiful baby daughter is now nearly a year old; it's a world where I am sleep-deprived (instead of in the constant state of medicinally induced hibernation that I sink into in my real life, popping a pill and retreating into blessed oblivion whenever I can); I walk up and down in the nursery when the rest of the world is asleep, holding her against my heart, stroking her back, soothing her and singing her lullabies, not minding that she won't go back to sleep, because her every breath, her every cry, is proof she's alive. In this other life, I deal cheerfully with dirty diapers, teething and tantrums, late night feeds and early morning wake-up calls; I plan her first Christmas—our first Christmas as a family—and her first birthday party; I chat to my sister, Tess, every day just like we used to do, offering her my sympathy and advice as her own pregnancy progresses, looking forward to the day when our children will be favourite cousins and spend magical summer holidays together at the lake house in New Hampshire.

You have to admit, it's a much nicer life than the real one.

So, when I'm alone, I allow myself to go there sometimes, luxuriating in the fantasy. Because, don't worry, I *do* know it's a fantasy. I've not yet taken to playing with dolls and pushing an empty buggy through the streets, cooing to my imaginary baby. It's my secret craziness, my own *Silver Linings Playbook*, where everything has turned out just fine in the end and Will and I are busy living in our own happy-ever-after.

Sad, isn't it, my private parallel universe? A refuge for my broken heart; a refuge from my grief.

The hall clock chimes. Shocked out of my reverie, I look at my boots sitting there on the doormat, and then catch a glimpse of my face in the hallway mirror. My skin is too pale and the dark half-moon shadows beneath my eyes stand out stark against it. I run a hand through my hair, trying to smooth the copper curls which have gone a little frizzy, as usual, in the damp London air.

I go upstairs to the bathroom, the two his-and-hers sinks mocking me as I rummage in the cabinet for the foil pack of pills. The doctor prescribed these antidepressants when I got to the stage of being unable to haul my sorry carcass out of bed for several days at a stretch. They make me feel a little foggy, removed from reality, but then isn't that the point? Under the unforgiving glare of the bathroom lights, my reflection seems too far away, as though it, too, has disconnected itself from me and my grief.

I guess you know you are really and truly alone when even your own reflection deserts you.

I sway a little, gripping the side of the sink to try to steady the faint giddiness as the pills kick in.

'*France*,' I whisper to myself again. A faint glimmer of light at the end of a very long, very dark, very lonely tunnel.

Chapter 2
Jingle Bells

A day or two ago
I thought I'd take a ride...

Sending up a little prayer of thanks for having survived the Parisian traffic, I swing the car into the underground parking lot at Sèvres-Babylone, stretch across the passenger seat to grab the ticket that the machine spits out, and manoeuvre gingerly into one of the narrow spaces. I sit for a moment in the sudden silence as the cooling motor ticks quietly and breathe out a big sigh of relief. As an American driving a British right-hand drive stick-shift car on the wrong side of the road (or, in fact, really the right side in *every* sense), I congratulate myself on having gotten this far safely, with only one near miss by a kamikaze taxi driver on the *p*ériphérique and just three aggressive blasts of the horn from French drivers sitting behind me at the stoplights a nanosecond after they turn green. Thank goodness for my GPS, whose endlessly patient and polite British tones have steered me here.

Emerging into the grey light of a Paris afternoon, I pause for a moment, orienting myself. When I first arrived in the city all those years ago, fresh off the plane from Boston and as green as the taste of a Key Lime Pie, it was a terrifying and bewildering city. But it soon became friendlier as I got the hang of the metro and worked out the geography of the place. The River Seine, the Eiffel Tower and Montmartre provided useful landmarks for newbies like me.

The *Bon Marché* beckons me, its name written boldly on the skyline in a thousand light bulbs, a vast emporium offering beautiful clothes and the best grocery store in the world bar none. I hitch my overnight bag onto my shoulder and stride out. I'll check in at the little hotel I've found, just off the Rue du Bac, and then head out again for a wander down my own personal Memory Lane...

I step out of the front door of the hotel, tentatively at first, but growing in confidence as more and more familiar places come back to me. I call in at the old-fashioned *Salon de Thé*–come–ice cream parlour with its red and gold storefront, for a cup of *tisane*, served in a thick white cup with a little almond cake—a *Cal-*

isson d'Aix—nestling on the saucer beside it. Then I stroll up the Rue du Bac, pausing often to gaze at the window displays in the little shops that line the street, at antiques and jewellery, furniture and flowers. The fish shop and the butcher's both stop me in my tracks for a good few minutes as I gaze at the bountiful displays of unfamiliar cuts of meat and strange creatures from the deep. Elegant Parisians, the men as smartly turned out and immaculately coiffed as the women, hurry in and out of the shops, small, wax-paper-wrapped packages of tempting morsels for dinner stowed into their designer purses (carried by the males as well as females). As I cross the Boulevard Saint-Germain, the streetlamps come on and car headlights stream by in a dizzying rip-tide of motion. I continue walking until I reach the river and cross the *quai* so that I can lean against the parapet and watch the Seine flow by. Brightly lit *bateaux mouches* churn the water into choppy chaos as they pass. The wind is brisker here, slicing through my jacket like a knife, so I pull the zipper up to my chin and turn and follow along beside the river, picking up the pace. It feels invigorating, despite the chill, to stretch my journey-stiffened limbs and breathe the cold air deep into my lungs. A faint scent of French fries and hot sugar wafts on the breeze: there must be a snack food stall up ahead.

As I round a corner, suddenly I find myself in a floodlit square. And Christmas ambushes me yet again!

It's a Breton market, colourful stalls selling laces and linens, crêpes and cider, waffles and *vin chaud*, and handcrafted wooden toys. Christmas lights are strung from stall to stall and French carols play from speakers hung amongst the twinkling fairy lights in the trees, filling the vanilla-and-spice-scented air with angelic music and the sound of sleigh bells. Families stroll and laugh, eating and drinking, and poring over the wares on offer. Buying toys for their children and lace-covered lavender bags for their grandmothers.

And, out of nowhere, my sadness comes crashing down around my ears.

I turn on my heel, stumbling against a woman pushing a baby in a stroller, apologising, panicking as the happy, festive crowd hems me in. I can't breathe. The smell of deep-fried food makes me sick to my stomach. I push my way to the sidewalk, step into the road looking the wrong way and jump out of my skin as a car horn blares loudly. The driver swerves, his wing mirror catching my elbow with a dull thud as he sweeps by.

A woman grabs me and pulls back to the safety of the sidewalk.

'*Madame? Etes-vous blessée?*' she enquires, concerned. People turn and stare, the woman with the stroller amongst them.

Am I hurt? Yes, I guess you could say I'm hurt. But the pain in my elbow—I flex it gingerly: bruised, but not broken, luckily—is nothing compared to the pounding in my head and the desperate empty ache in my heart.

'I'm okay. *Merci.*' I catch my breath, trying to blank out the jumble of images in my mind, of brightly painted wooden toys, soft linens, a drawer full of tiny knitted bootees in pastel colours, a brand-new stroller, never used, leaning against the wall in the hallway at home.

I manage to cross the street without getting myself killed and walk quickly back to the hotel. '*Stupid, stupid!*' I berate myself. Thinking it was that easy for you to escape. Thinking you could outrun the sadness. Thinking a few hours in Paris would cure the heartache and let you forget.

Still trembling, I collect my keys from the front desk of the hotel and climb the four flights of narrow stairs to my room. Up here, under the charcoal grey slates of the mansard roof, there's a view across the rooftops to where the tip of the Eiffel Tower winks and glitters with its brilliant show of lights. Just as it did all those years ago. Only now it's laughing *at* me, not *with* me. I cross quickly to the window and pull the curtains together, shutting it out. Then head to the bathroom, run water into a glass, swallow a couple of pills fast to dull the pain that's too much to bear.

Paris was a mistake. Too many memories. Too much risk of running headlong into Christmas just when you least expect it. I lie down on the bed in the darkened room, waiting for the fog of blessed, chemically induced numbness to descend. Tomorrow I'll leave early, as soon as the worst of the rush-hour traffic has died down. Heading west and then south, to the blissful isolation of the deepest French country-side where I'll be in control. No cars (my throbbing elbow is already turning a deep purple-black), no babies in strollers, and—most importantly of all—categorically no Christmas.

I've never been to the *Sud-Ouest* before, which is a pretty big omission given that one-quarter of my roots extend into the bedrock of this particular corner of France.

Mamie Lucie used to tell me stories of her child-hood in the Périgord, the region which lies just to the east of Rose and Max's holiday home, as we cooked together in her kitchen. As I stood on a chair at the kitchen table, an oversized apron tied around my middle to prevent too much flour getting onto my clothes while I rolled out a ball of sweet shortcrust pastry, she would reminisce about the rich farmland that surrounded her parents' home, the fields of sunflowers turning their obedient faces to follow the summer sun; orchards where red-black cherries and dark purple plums ripened, each in their own season; plantations of walnut and hazel trees, as old as her own grandparents, whose rich brown kernels were gathered each fall; vineyards where trellised vines spread their arms wide in the sunshine, drinking it in to sweeten their clusters of ripening grapes in time for the wine harvest. It was from her that I learned about the importance of cooking with the best seasonal produce. In the depths of the New England winter, my mother, rebelling no doubt, would casually throw green beans from Kenya and raspberries from Chile into her basket at Shaw's, with little regard for either flavour or cost. And *Mamie* Lucie would tut and shake her head, and produce a pumpkin pie, or a *Tarte Tatin* made with crisp McIntosh apples from Vermont, or a dish of roasted root vegetables infused with garlic and rosemary that would make our taste buds perform cartwheels of joy, the ingredients bought from the local farmers' market.

In the first few days of December each year—so right about now in fact—there'd be a special cookery session. 'Evie, Tess, *allons-y*! It's time to do our baking for Saint Nicolas.' We'd get out the big cream mixing bowl, its glaze crackled with age, and our rolling pins (an old, heavy oak one for *Mamie* Lucie and smaller, more manageable beech-wood ones that she'd bought for my sister and me), and mix together the butter, sugar and spices to make the cookies for the saint's feast day on the sixth of the month. First we'd make the star-shaped *bredeles* and Tess and I would decorate them with brown hazelnuts and sugared orange peel, and then we'd prepare the dough for the gingerbread men. *Mamie* Lucie's special recipe, which was passed down to her by her own mother—who was originally from Alsace in the north of France, where celebrating the feast of Saint Nicolas is almost a bigger deal than Christmas itself—included adding little nuggets of succulent crystallised ginger which exploded with flavour as we bit into the finished cookies that had been drizzled with white sugar frosting.

'Tell us about the Bad Butcher again,' we'd implore as we cut the shapes from the cookie dough, nibbling on the raw scraps until our grandmother stopped us, saying we'd get a stomach ache.

'Well, my darlings, a very, very long time ago and a very, very long way away, there lived a very, very bad butcher. One day, three little children wandered away from their mothers and got lost. Cold and hungry, they came to a butcher's shop where they begged for shelter. But the bad butcher took them—*un, deux, trois*—and cut them up with his big, sharp knife and popped them into his brine pot.' Our eyes would grow as big as saucers at this point in the story and Tess and I would shiver with delighted horror at the gruesome tale, safe in the knowledge of a happy ending.

'But then, one winter's day, seven long years later, Saint Nicolas came to the butcher's shop and, in his turn, asked the man for shelter. "But of course; do come in," said the butcher. "May I have something to eat as well?" asked the saint. "Certainly, Saint Nicolas! Would you like a little piece of this ham? Or perhaps this veal?" "No, thank you," replied the saint. "I'd like the meat that you've been keeping in your brine pot these past seven years." Upon hearing this, the bad butcher ran away, terrified. The saint placed his hand on the rim of the brine pot *et hop!*—*un, deux, trois*—the three children leapt out, as right as rain. And to this day, the saint comes back on the sixth of

December every year and gives good little children gifts and cookies. But you'd better watch out for the bad butcher—*Le Père Fouettard*—who comes behind him, in shame, leaving nothing but bundles of twigs for children who have been naughty.'

After our baking session, we'd be allowed just one of the sweet, melting cookies—'As long as you've been good little girls?' *Mamie* Lucie would ask, her eyes smiling with love behind her mock-stern expression. The rest would be saved for the Saint's day when, next to our shoes which had been filled with candy, little baskets of gifts and the cookies would magically appear on the front porch, with labels inscribed to 'Miss Evie Callahan' and 'Miss Tess Callahan' tied to the handles with red-and-white ribbons. We were the envy of our school friends when we shared our spoils with them, having our Saint Nicolas treats to tide us over so fortuitously between Thanksgiving and Christmas.

I must still have the recipes for the cookies in *Mamie*'s notebook, which I've brought with me on my road trip back to her homeland.

One of these days I'll look them out.

Not this year. But one day...

Rose has shown me photographs of their French holiday home. It looks positively idyllic: an old stone farmhouse with a red-tiled roof. In the pictures, the sun is always shining and there are pots of red geraniums and a spectacular, sprawling vine covered in flame-coloured trumpet-like flowers which casts its shade onto a terrace behind the house. Of course, they're usually here in the summer, so I'm not expecting it to be quite so lush at this time of year. But, I have to admit, my heart sinks a little as the GPS tells me I'm nearing my destination. To be honest, the landscape is, well, a bit bleak. Bare trees stand stark under a lead-grey sky and in the vineyards the vine stocks are grotesque, wizened stumps. Apart from the grass which grows in a thick carpet along the roadside, the only greenery is the parasitic mistletoe that hangs in the branches of the trees, dark lace pompoms like ink blots against the sheet of winter clouds.

I try to recall what Rose told me when she was describing how to recognise their house. 'You'll see the little white signpost for *Les Pèlerins*. It means "The Pilgrims", because it's on one of the pilgrim routes to Santiago de Compostela that wind through France and all the way across the northern coast of Spain. Look out for the cockleshell way-markers and you'll know you're getting near. Occasionally you still see pilgrims walking up the lane, though I doubt there'll be any in the winter. It's a tiny hamlet, just a handful of buildings. On the right-hand side is the cottage belonging to our neighbours Mathieu and Eliane—you'll see a gateway to a château just beyond it. On the left-hand side there's a cluster of buildings, two houses, some outbuildings and a big barn. Ours is the first house you come to when you drive into the courtyard, the one with two big oak trees beside it. The other one belongs to old Doctor Lebrun and his wife, Anne. The neighbours are all charming, but Mathieu and Eliane are ancient and the doctor and his wife must be well into their sixties now. So all in all it's a good thing you're not going for the hectic social life! Your arrival is going to lower the average age of the inhabitants of *Les Pélérins* by a long chalk.'

She'd continued, 'I spoke to Eliane yesterday and let her know you're coming, so that Mathieu can open the shutters and have the water turned back on for your arrival. Ask them if there's anything you're not certain about. Are you sure you'll be okay there with no heating? There's a good supply of logs in the woodshed though.'

'Don't worry, I'll be fine,' I assured her. 'I'll take warm clothes; after all, I'm used to New England winters which make your sorry British efforts look like a balmy spring day.'

And surely, I think, having driven south for two days solid, the weather must be even milder in south-west France? I'm relishing the thought of sitting snugly beside a crackling fire, catching up on reading the lengthy list of books that I've got lined up on my iPad. Or taking long, revitalising walks in the French winter sunshine, breathing the London pollution out of my lungs. It's going to be bliss!

Here's the signpost now. The tiny hamlet of *Les Pélérins* huddles beneath the lowering sky, and I see the twin oaks, adorned with mistletoe pompoms of their own, their bare branches stirring in the winter wind, beckoning me on in.

I find the key under a stone beside the front door, just as Rose has described. The lock is stiff and the door opens on its rusted hinges with a drawn-out creak. I step into a long, narrow hallway that runs the length of the house, a staircase at the far end leading to bedrooms under the roof. In the late after-noon, the thick stone walls don't allow much light in through the windows whose panes are misty with winter dust. The desiccated bodies of dead flies dot the low windowsills and the air inside the house is almost as chill and damp as it is outside. Tall, pan-elled doors, their closed faces inscrutable, lead off the hallway. I push the first one open and step into a long, light sitting room where someone—Mathieu when he was opening the shutters, I guess—has laid a fire in the hearth ready for lighting. Quickly, before the dampness and the chill and the grey afternoon can impose themselves on my mood any further, I strike a match from the box on the mantelpiece and hold the tiny flame to an edge of newspaper in the grate. It flickers, catches, creeps in under the kindling and, gratifyingly easily, begins to take hold of the dry sticks that crackle and pop, instantly cheering both the room and me.

I gaze about myself, taking stock of my surroundings. This room has tall French doors and their window panes let light flood in, despite the lack of sunshine today. They lead to a terrace outside where, I imagine, the orange-flowered vine casts its shade in the summer. The floor of the room is of old wooden boards, polished to a soft patina with age and beeswax, and several rag rugs add splashes of colour. Two soft, deep sofas flank the fireplace, covered with a once-fine floral chintz which has faded and worn with use, the arms threadbare. On a console table pushed against one wall stand a cluster of framed photographs and I cross to take a closer look, smiling at the familiar faces of Rose, Max and their boys that grin out at me from the pictures. The photos are full of sun and laughter, holiday-time snaps of tanned skin and heat and freedom from the routines of work and school. 'Am I pleased to see you guys!' I exclaim, my voice loud in the silence which is relieved only by the soft muttering of the fire as it begins to burn more steadily, radiating a gentle but encouraging heat.

I go back into the hallway, leaving the sitting room door open to allow the light and warmth to filter into the rest of the house, driving out the shadows and the faint mustiness of the air that has been shut in here since the end of the summer. I push open the other doors, exploring. Next to the sitting room is another long, spacious room which, from the look of its uneven beams, appears to have originally been two smaller rooms that have been knocked through to create a generous dining kitchen. An ancient cast-iron range dominates the far end. It's clearly just for decoration as there's a more modern electric hob and oven set into the cream Shaker-style cabinets that are fitted around the walls. Cheerful red gingham curtains frame the windows, and there's another set of French doors leading out to the garden terrace beyond. A scrubbed pine table and chairs are set before these doors to take advantage of the view. It must be spectacular in summer. The garden, where shrubby rosemary and bay bushes spread their leaves to the grey winter sky in search of sunshine, slopes gently at first and then falls away more steeply as the hillside plunges headlong towards the broad silver river in the valley below. On one side there's a sloping meadow, where a white horse is calmly cropping the lush winter grass, and on the other a vineyard, whose neat rows of trellising hug the contours of the land.

In the middle of the lawn—if the rough grass beyond the terrace can be called that—stands a bizarre sight: it's an ancient apple tree, its trunk twisted and gnarled with age, and its branches have lost every single one of their leaves; but rust-red apples still hang from them, points of colour in the grey landscape. And, if it weren't for the fact that such things are completely banned this year, I would say they look exactly like the baubles on a Christmas tree. A robin hops on the ground amongst a few windfalls beneath the tree and then, as I watch, it flutters up and perches on the tip of the very highest twig, cocking its head and flaunting its russet breast, looking, for all the world, as though it's laughing at me. Or, perhaps, inviting me to laugh along with it. As non-Christmas trees go, it's really a very pretty sight. I smile. My spirits pick up a little and I think, *'Plan B will do very nicely indeed, thank you, Rose and Max.'*

I feel cocooned here, far enough away, at last, from London with its constant reminders of failure and disappointment and loss; far enough away from Paris and its bustle and busyness, its memories of a stage of my life that's now long gone; far enough away from my family in Boston to allow them the space to stop worrying about me and enjoy their lives, unimpeded by the weight of my sorrow; far enough from the magazine articles and the TV programmes and, at last, far enough away from Christmas itself.

Going out to the car to start bringing in my cases, I pause in the doorway for a moment, listening. The only sound is the faint sigh of the winter wind as it brushes past the bare branches of the oak trees, making the fronds of mistletoe stir and shiver. Nothing more. Now, finally, in this vacuum of space and quietness, where I know no one and no one expects anything of me, I think I just might be able to find some kind of peace of mind at last.

Chapter 3
The Twelve Days of Christmas

On the third day of Christmas, my true love sent to me
Three French hens...

Aargh! That does it; I swear I'm going to wring that rooster's neck and make him into a tasty *coq au vin*. Right after I've wrung the neck of the other bird, whatever it is—some kind of owl, I guess—that woke me up in the middle of the night with its screeching, leaving me lying in the pitch darkness (a much darker darkness than any I've been used to in cities), with my heart pounding and my mouth dry. The bird's startlingly loud scream seemed to come from one of the oak trees just beyond the wall of my bedroom.

I pulled the covers up round my ears, shutting out the cold night air as well as the noise of the neighbour's dog which was also now barking enthusiastically. Once that finally stopped, I lay awake for a while, eyes wide in the darkness, waiting for the welcome oblivion of sleep to return. And then, no sooner had I finally dropped off again than that rooster decided it was time to sound the morning alarm. I reach a hand out from the cosiness of the covers and grope on the bedside cabinet for my watch. Squinting to read the dial in the first, very faint light of the dawn that's just beginning to filter in through the skylight above my head, I make out that it's barely six. I turn over, pulling the covers back up again, reluctant to leave the warmth of my bed. Even a short trip to the bathroom entails a scramble to pull on my thick sweater and long woollen socks before shoving my feet into my slippers. The floorboards are cold enough but the bathroom tiles are positively glacial.

It turns out that the peace and quiet of the countryside is a whole lot noisier than I'd ever have imagined. The first night I was here I turned in early, worn out after the long drive as well as all the emotion of leaving London and visiting Paris. I'd heard what I guessed must be the doctor's car pulling up in front of the house next door, the quiet slam of the door and the crunch of footsteps on the gravel. I'd held my breath for a moment, wondering whether he and his wife, noticing the smoke rising from the chimney, would feel obliged to come and knock on my front door to say hello. But it was already on the late side for a social call, and all my lights were off, and thankfully the footsteps made their way in the opposite direction. A door opened, then closed with a firm thud. And then I lay and listened, with intrigue at first and then with increasing irritation as, from one of the outbuildings, sounds of distant sawing, then hammering, then the whirr of a drill rudely interrupted the drowsiness that had begun to soothe my frayed nerves in the pleasant aftermath of a cup of camomile tea and a hot bath. The last thing I remembered thinking was, *'How very inconsiderate; now I'll never get to sleep!'* before dropping off a cliff into deep, dark oblivion. And by the time that darned screech owl woke me again in the wee small hours, the sounds from the garage had fallen silent. I suppose I should have been thankful for small mercies.

The next morning I'd set off to call on my two sets of neighbours, thinking I should go introduce myself for politeness' sake. There was no car outside the doctor's house—he must already have gone to work, I guessed—but I knocked at the door hoping his wife might be in. The house was firmly locked up though, as was the garage. (Okay, I admit I tried the door, hoping to get a peek into the late-night workshop, but the panes of glass were too heavily frosted for me to be able to make out anything inside.) I passed the woodshed with its neatly stacked log pile, and stuck my head into the barn, where the white horse peered at me over the top of its stable door. 'Well, hello there,' I said, surprised to see it here instead of in the field at the back of the house. It must have been brought in yesterday evening, out of the frosty night air. 'Sorry, I've nothing for you. I'll bring you an apple next time, I promise.' The horse, evidently unimpressed, snorted and turned back to pull some wisps of sweet-smelling hay from the wooden manger on the far wall.

I crossed the lane, making my way to Eliane and Mathieu's house, which had a promising plume of wood-smoke drifting above one of its chimneys. But, although I knocked and called at the front door, and even tentatively walked around to the back of the house and called there, there was no sign of anyone. A robin, maybe the same one from the apple tree the day before, hopped onto a clod of earth in the middle of a neat vegetable patch and then flew up to perch on the handle of a garden fork that was stuck into the rich, freshly dug soil. Dark green cabbages rested in the bed next to taller, knobbly Brussels sprouts, and leeks whose neatly braided leaves ended in foun-tain-like flourishes. Not wanting to trespass further, I left, resolving to call again another day—though in truth I was a little relieved too, still relishing the sense of being alone and not having to make conversational small talk with anyone for a while. My new neighbours haven't approached me in the days since then either; clearly French country-folk are happy to respect one another's space.

The rooster crows again, twice over this time, as if he knows his first attempt to sound *reveille* didn't succeed in getting me out from under the covers. I sigh deeply, still determined not to be bullied into getting up before I'm good and ready. To tell the truth, I'd rather try and sleep a bit longer because, otherwise, I know how the day will stretch out, dauntingly long, ahead of me. If I could, I'd stay under the covers, like a hibernating bear, until Christmas is safely behind me and it's safe to come out, blinking in the spring sunshine.

The first few days here were fine. I was happy to pass the time unpacking and getting myself settled in, slowly getting familiar with my new surroundings, mastering the art of setting and lighting the fire, curling up on one of the sofas to read for hours on end, relishing my solitude. Not having to think. But already I can see that time may start to drag and I fear a return of the depression that may roll back in at any moment. It sits out there, like a fog bank off the

Maine coast. The distraction of a new place can only hold it at bay for a short time, I know. So, despite Foghorn Leghorn over the way, I'm determined to try to doze a while longer. Then, because Rose told me Saturday is market day there, I'm planning on taking myself down to Sainte-Foy-La-Grande. Just to give myself something to do. And also because I know I really need to make myself eat something other than the cans of soup and crackers I've been resorting to for the past few days since my arrival here. *Mamie* Lucie's recipe book sits on the table in the kitchen, looking at me reproachfully as I spoon bright orange gloop into a pan to heat through. One of these days, I tell it, I'll cook something proper, I promise...

Still under the covers, I close my eyes, hoping to slip back into blessed unconsciousness once again, but then immediately open them again, wide with fear... Because there's a strange, furtive noise coming from just outside the house. It sounds like someone's tip-toeing across the gravel, breathing heavily. The only windows up here are roof lights, so I can't peek out at the intruder, who pauses every now and then—I imagine him trying the front door and the windows downstairs—before the footsteps tiptoe round the end of the house. Oh no, now he's on the other side... I can hear that heavy breathing, and soft footfalls crossing the grass. He's going to break in through one of the sets of French doors. Will the doctor and his wife hear him? If they're that old, then probably not. Will they hear if I scream? They're probably still fast asleep this early on a Saturday morning.

I'm panicking now, my own breath coming fast and shallow. Surely it'll be better to confront him downstairs while he's still outside—and with my thick sweater on instead of just in my pyjamas—than wait until he's in the house? Quickly and quietly I pull on my layers of warmer clothes and creep downstairs. Moving swiftly and silently into the kitchen, I grab a large breadknife and cross to the terrace doors, preparing to brandish the knife and scream at the top of my lungs in the hope of creating such a disturbance that the intruder will flee in terror. Used to city life, I usually carry a canister of pepper spray in my purse, but I jettisoned this before I left London, thinking I wouldn't need such things in the safe, tranquil French countryside. How I regret that now! So instead I snatch up the pepper pot from the table, thinking at least it's better than nothing.

A dense white fog has closed in overnight. Its chill has turned the air itself into a solid wall of blankness, obscuring the rest of the world so that I feel even more isolated than ever.

And then I freeze in my tracks—freeze being the operative word on this frigid December morning—at the sight before me. Under the apple tree, which emerges out of the fog like a phantom, stands the most enormous pig I've ever seen, gazing longingly up at the apples still hanging from the branches. I tap on the glass and it peers short-sightedly towards the house, then, not the least bit bothered by my presence—and disdainfully ignoring the fact that I seem to be threatening it with two items of kitchen equipment better suited to making a ham sandwich than to actual self-defence—it begins to root blissfully amongst the fallen fruit, crunching the rotting apples between its large, ivory teeth.

I put my hands on my hips and shake my head in exasperation. So much for rural tranquillity! Between the crowing rooster, the screeching owl, the barking dog, the midnight mechanic and now this hungry hog, the chance of a little peace and quiet would be a very fine thing indeed.

I tap on the window pane again, harder this time, but the pig doesn't even look up. So I unbolt the French doors and, grasping the breadknife and pepper pot in what I imagine to be a fearsome fashion—showing this critter I mean business—I step out onto the terrace.

I realise two things in quick succession: fortunately the far side is bounded by a low wall which would offer some protection if the pig decided to charge; and unfortunately the flagstones of the terrace are covered in a carpet of dead leaves which have become slick with the saturating dampness of the fog. My feet slide out from underneath me and, giving a loud yell, I land on my behind with a thud that knocks the wind out of me momentarily. I heave myself up, hanging on to the wall for dear life, and rub my right hip, which took the brunt of the fall. My shout, and the clattering of breadknife and pepper pot onto the flagstones, hardly disturbed the pig at all. He looks at me appraisingly, his little eyes blinking as he chews an especially delicious rotten apple, and then nonchalantly turns his back on me and goes back to rooting in the damp grass for more booty.

I collect up my scattered weapons, sliding wildly again and windmilling my arms in a most inelegant manner, before retreating inside. As I turn back towards the house, I notice a movement behind an upstairs window at the doctor's house, as if someone has drawn back from the glass from where they've been watching my escapades. Great. Now my elderly neighbours know that a crazed knife-wielding pig attacker has moved in next door to them. I do so love to create a good first impression! They've also witnessed my fall, no doubt, so my pride now hurts almost as much as my backside does.

Admitting defeat on the pig-scaring front, I replace the pepper pot and the knife beside the breadboard on the kitchen counter and stomp back upstairs to get dressed properly.

As I brush my hair, I catch sight of myself in the bathroom mirror and I notice the faint frown lines that have etched themselves between my brows. When did that happen? I pause, hairbrush in hand, suddenly remembering the expression of serene disdain on the face of the pig as it surveyed the city slicker brandishing the pepper pot and breadknife at it, and I start to laugh.

And as my reflection laughs back at me, she looks relieved that, after such a long absence, it turns out her owner's sense of humour hasn't upped and left for good after all.

◆ ◆ ◆

The pig has disappeared into the fog by the time I've brushed my teeth, peeled off my layers of nightwear (gingerly pressing on the large red circle on my hip where I fell, which is already beginning to darken to a becoming shade of purple that matches the bruise on my elbow), and pulled on my jeans, a thermal under-shirt and several more layers of sweaters. I make a pot of coffee and cup my hands around the mug to warm them as I sit at the kitchen table, gazing out at the wall of whiteness.

The crisp winter sunshine that I'd envisaged has failed entirely to materialise so far. I can't even check out a weather forecast as the Internet isn't working. There's a very faint network signal, but the password Rose gave me doesn't seem to allow me access. After a bit of a hunt I've discovered the router, which is under the console table in the sitting room but, despite the fact that it's plugged into the mains, its lights are all off. I pick up my phone, hoping against hope, but I can't get any reception on that here either. One of these days I'll have to try walking to the top of the hill to see if I can get any signal up there. But so far I haven't bothered. I'll take it with me to the market though and hopefully be able to pick up a network in Sainte-Foy.

It's weird being so disconnected from everything and everyone. All at once the lack of communica-tion with the outside world and the—no doubt complicated—technicalities that will be involved in restoring it, overwhelm me. Suddenly exhaustion crushes my spirit and doubts come crashing in.

How could I ever have thought I could do this? For a moment I toy with the idea of loading everything back into the car and heading back to London. I could do that easily: run back home to the warmth and familiarity of my own house; spend Christmas with Rose and Max, or even—there's still time—get a flight back to the States. I smile wryly and take another sip of my coffee. As that pig out there must have believed, it's certainly true that the grass always seems greener on the other side of the fence. In reality, I know that what awaits me back in London is a silence and an emptiness even more profound than the one I find myself in here. All those reminders of what should have been. I realise that, in the few days I've been here, I have at least stopped living in that other, parallel life, my make-believe happy-ever-after. And I haven't popped a pill in days. So even if it's foggy outside, my internal fogginess is beginning to lift a little. That sense of seeing the world from behind a plate of glass has evaporated into thin air now that the novelty of a new place has reconnected me with Planet Earth, my feet more firmly planted on the cold French ground.

And even though I haven't once turned a page, *Mamie* Lucie's notebook still sits there on the table in front of me, waiting expectantly. It's strange that a simple, inanimate object can have such a powerful effect, constantly reminding me of that side of my life which I now seem to be incapable of resuming. I sigh. *I'm getting there, Mamie, I promise.*

Rousing myself for action instead of wallowing in my thoughts, I go back upstairs to fetch my bag and the car keys. I think I hear the faint crunch of footsteps on the gravel: that darned pig again, no doubt. I throw open the front door, ready to confront the beast and shoo it away, but there's nothing there.

With a strangely disconcerting swirl, as though some presence has just disturbed it, the fog shifts, seeming about to clear, but then closing in again. It makes me feel a little giddy and I put a hand out to steady myself against the door frame. As I do so, I glance down, my peripheral vision caught by a flash of red. And there on the doorstep sits a little basket tied with a jaunty red bow. I gasp, remembering the Saint Nicolas gifts from my childhood. Thinking hard, I try to recall what today's date must be. It's Saturday, the first one in December. So it must be the sixth! Stooping to pick up the basket, I see there's a slip of paper tucked in beneath the wrappings. '*Bienvenue*' it reads. Nothing more. I peel back a sheet of baking parchment and there, nestling beneath it, discover a little cache of star-shaped cookies, iced with white frosting. I bend my head and breathe in deeply, inhaling the familiar scent of butter and spice.

'*Merci*, Saint Nicolas,' I say, my words hanging in the air until the fog, shifting and swirling once again, swallows them up.

I set the basket on the table in the kitchen, next to *Mamie* Lucie's recipe book. Still clasping my car keys, I stand for a moment with my hands on my hips again, taking in the festive red bow, the sweet-smelling cookies and the notebook beside them. And suddenly I don't feel at all alone after all.

'Okay, *Mamie*, I get the message. Let's go see what the market has to offer.'

I creep down the steep hill in the car, headlights on, hugging the right-hand verge. The fog grows even thicker as I find a parking place next to the river in the little town of Sainte-Foy. On the passenger seat next to me, my phone suddenly pings, picking up a signal, incoming text messages lighting up the screen.

There's a cheerful one from my mother—'hope u got there ok. Do u have email? If not txt back. All fine here xx'—and then several increasingly anxious ones from Rose. I punch in her number, smiling at her gleeful screech as she picks up. '*There* you are!

I've been worried about you with this radio silence. Is everything okay? I ended up phoning Eliane to make sure you'd actually got there.'

'I'm fine, it's all fine, Rose. So lovely to hear your voice! The house is great. But I can't get a signal on my phone there and the Internet seems to be down.' I describe the sorry state of the Wi-Fi router to her.

'Oh God, what a pain. Sorry, Evie, it sounds like it's been fried in a winter storm. The same thing happened once before. I'm not sure what to suggest. It's probably going to mean a trip to Bordeaux or Bergerac to buy a whole new router. And then you'd need to install it of course...'

'Don't worry; I'm happy to make do without it. And now that I know I can get a signal down here, I can check emails and make calls when I come to do my shopping. It's taken me a few days to get settled in, is all. This is my first time venturing forth!'

'Okay, well, if you're sure. Sorry—I can't think of anyone else there we could ask to help you. Your neighbours are all of the pre-Internet generation, I'm afraid. Oh, and you'll probably also get a signal if you go up the road above the house up to the top of the hill. Just follow the cockleshell markers for the pilgrim way—they'll take you in the right direction.'

'Great. I'll try that too. I'm going to get into a routine of daily walks now. As soon as the weather picks up a bit, that is. Don't worry; I promise I'll stay in touch from here on in.'

I sit in the car a while longer, checking emails and composing a reassuringly cheery reply to my mom. The fog alternately retreats teasingly out across the broad, brown river and then closes back in again. There's nothing from Will. I thought there might be a reply to the brief, business-like message I'd sent him before I left England to let him know I'd be away until early January, telling him where I am. Just in case... I even managed to wish him luck with his TV launch. But he's clearly far too busy and far too important these days. Or too distracted by mystery girl Stephanie Whatsername perhaps.

I gather up my purse and a large straw basket that I've borrowed from the house and step out into the mist, following the flow of people heading for the marketplace in the middle of town. The narrow streets open out suddenly into a space that is filled with a bustling throng. Colourful market stalls are clustered around the imposing *Mairie* that dominates the square. I stand still for a moment, people pushing busily past me, and I feel a little overwhelmed by so much sensory overload after the past few days of self-imposed solitary confinement.

The noise is the first thing I notice. Voices jabber and call, and I'm assailed on all sides by quick-fire French, spoken with an accent very different to that of the Parisians. Progress into the *place* is slow, as people greet one another and then linger in clusters, catching up with the latest gossip, the storm of chatter interspersed with frequent gusts of laughter.

Then my eyes open wide as I take in the produce on offer. If there's a heaven where my grandmother has gone, then I imagine it must look a lot like this. Fruit and vegetables are displayed in neat pyramids, bright orange and yellow citrus fruits contrasting with the more sombre, leathery green leaves of cabbages and something called *blette*, which I realise is Swiss chard. Sunny orange carrots are eclipsed by a staggering array of squashes in all shapes and sizes, mottled yellow turban squash, gnarled grey-green Hubbards and flame-coloured pumpkins. In contrast, the neighbouring fish stall is a study in understated elegance, muted shades of silver and black scales reclining on a sumptuous bed of crushed ice; midnight blue mussels nestle among tendrils of glossy brown seaweed, with a shoal of coral-pink prawns adding a dash of colour.

Noticing a heap of the little clams we call steamers back home, I pause, contemplating; I could buy some to make a proper New England chowder, the perfect creamy comfort food for this winter weather, or perhaps cook them the French way with some white wine and shallots, using *Mamie* Lucie's recipe which must be in her notebook somewhere… Food for thought, quite literally.

Next, I stand stock still outside a *pâtisserie*, whose fuchsia-pink shopfront frames a feast of jewel-like confections, a neatly arranged, close-packed patchwork of *gâteaux* and *tartelettes,* glowing with golden pastry, ruby fruit and dark velvety chocolate, alongside a towering pyramid of pretty pastel-coloured macaroons.

I made a conical tower of macaroons like that for our wedding cake, colouring some palest gold to contrast with the pure white of the others. I decorated the cake stand with a swathe of star-flowered jasmine and tied a wide gold ribbon in a bow around the base.

I remember Will patiently helping break dozens of eggs and separating the whites into a mixing bowl for me, then conjuring up a big batch of home-made mayonnaise with the left-over yolks, trickling golden-green olive oil from a height like a magician as he whisked the emulsion with the other hand.

He could always make me smile, once upon a time.

And I'm smiling now, I realise, as I catch a glimpse of my face reflected in the window of the *pâtisserie*, happy in my memories of the way we used to express our love through creating and sharing good food together.

I tear myself away, turning back to the market-place behind me. And now my sense of smell goes into overdrive: I pause here and there to inhale the delicious, faintly mould-tinged scent from the cheese stall, where soft white goats' cheeses jostle for position between wheels of hard yellow *brébis* and a vast, generously gooey *Brie de Meaux*; the bitter-salt smell of olives in their brine; garlicky dried sausage and—most heavenly of all—sizzling chickens turning slowly on a rotisserie, dripping their golden juices onto a layer of diced potatoes below, portions of which will be scooped into waxed paper bags and taken home for Saturday lunch as the market draws to a close.

I breathe in the scent of hot fat, but hurry on past as a faint tinge of nausea makes my stomach growl. It's been several days since I ate a proper meal, so I guess it might be best to ease myself back in gently. I head back to the fish stall and buy a sea-bass fillet, planning to sear it so that the skin turns a crisp sil-ver-black on top of the firm white flesh. I'll serve it with some creamed potatoes and steamed *blette*, with a little butter melting over the dark green leaves. Totally simple and totally delicious.

Next door there's a whole stall dedicated to oysters; rows of baskets are filled to the brim with the slate-black shellfish, and there's a quite bewildering range of choice, as each crate is individually labelled by size and origin. Would one choose the size 3 from the Ile d'Oléron or would the larger size 2 from the Bassin d'Arcachon be better? I'm not sure I feel like being that adventurous today, but perhaps I could plan to start off with half a dozen for my Christmas lunch. Not that I'm going to be celebrating Christmas, of course, but it could be a good excuse to devise a French-style menu for myself at a time when the very best produce is on offer. I decide I'll make a few notes and maybe browse through *Mamie* Lucie's notebook when I get home, seeking further inspiration.

I linger and loiter, enjoying standing in line as it gives me time to take in the bewildering range of produce and plan possible recipes. I haven't felt inspired like this in the longest time. *Mamie* would be proud of me, asking about unfamiliar ingredients, my French beginning to come back to me with growing confidence. You only have to ask a French stallholder for advice about how to cook his wares and you'll find yourself engaged in a lengthy and detailed explanation, with frequent interruptions, interjections and contradictions from everyone else in the line around you. Note that I say 'around you' rather than 'behind you'. Because there's nothing line-like about the way the French stand in line; it's more of a loose cluster. But the stallholders seem to have a way of knowing exactly who got there first, and if they lose track then there'll be a general debate to ascertain whose turn it is to be served next.

My purchases safely stowed into my basket, I meander slowly back through the crowded streets towards the river. I feel drained suddenly, my legs like lead weights. *That'll teach you to laze around doing nothing all day,* I chide myself. It's high time I started making more of an effort. Proper food and more exercise from here on in, I resolve.

As I pass the church that dominates one corner of the square, its steeple disappearing upwards into the fog, the door opens and a man hurries out leaving it ajar, allowing the sound of music to escape behind him. I climb the stone steps, thinking at first that I'll just pull the door closed from a sense of civic duty, but as I reach it a woman appears and opens it a little wider, ushering me in. The air inside is still and dry in comparison with the swirling mist outside, and a faintly spicy scent of incense hangs there like an invisible veil. I sink down thankfully onto a wooden pew at the very back of the church and set down the heavy basket; I'll just rest my tired legs for a few minutes and then I'll slip away. The woman reappears at my side, smiles and silently hands me a printed service sheet. She gestures to show me that it's translated into English on the other side, and I smile back a little ruefully: why is it that the French *always* know that you're a foreigner, even without a word being said? Though I guess, in my case, the mane of unruly russet curls and the pale East Coast complexion give it away every time.

A young priest is conducting a choir of children at the front of the church, accompanied by an organist. I close my eyes for a moment, resting and letting the music wash over me. Then the priest gestures for the choir to sit, and he begins to speak.

I open my eyes when I hear the words '*Saint Nicolas*'... Of course! This must be a special service for the Saint's feast day. I hope all of these children have woken this morning to find their shoes filled with cookies, candy and coins. I smile as I remember the basket of baking that awaits me back at the house. Rose said she'd called and spoken to Eliane, so I guess *she* must be the Secret Santa. Or, rather, Secret

Saint Nicolas, which amounts to the same thing. I'll go try her door again this afternoon to thank her.

His sermon over, the priest gestures for the children to stand again and the first notes of the final song ring out on the organ. It's a beautiful, plaintive melody and I turn over the service sheet so that I can follow the words.

'*Ils* étaient *trois petits enfants…*' the children sing. '*There were three little children…*' It's the story of the Bad Butcher! I follow the verses, flipping the page over for the translation every now and then. And then it comes to the final verse, when the Saint brings the three children back to life.

And my eyes suddenly fill with tears.

'*Saint Nicolas placed three fingers on the rim of the brine tub.*

The first child said, "I slept so well!"

The second said, "And so did I!"

The littlest one added, "I thought I was in paradise!"'

The children's pure voices cease and the organ sighs its last notes into the incense-scented air of the church.

I sit there, as the congregation files out into the bustle of the market square, going home to their Saturday lunches of roast chicken and Saint Nicolas Day *brioche*, and I bend my head and cry and cry. At long last, after so many months of dry-eyed silence, the floodgates open, here in this little church so far from anything and anyone I know, unlocked by the Saint Nicolas Day song and the memories of my *Mamie* Lucie's love that suddenly seem clearer than they ever have before.

After a while, the church falls silent, the final footfalls dying away.

I raise my head, and realise that I'm not alone in the last pew at the very back. A small figure in a black cassock has slipped in at the other end and sits quietly, his hands clasped on the back of the pew in front of us as if in prayer. My breathing begins to even out again, the storm of my emotions blowing over, and I gather my coat around me, preparing to leave. The young priest turns and smiles at me, then slides along the pew, closer to where I'm sitting.

'*Madame*, please, you don't have to hurry away. You are welcome to sit a while longer if you'd like. Get your strength back a little before you return to the world outside.' He fishes under his robes and pulls out a clean handkerchief which he passes to me. And then we sit together, in silence, he with his hands loosely clasped before him once again.

'I lost my baby,' I tell him when I can speak again, finally, and it's such a relief to be able to talk at last, to find the words to say the things I haven't been able to express until now. Perhaps it's because he's a stranger, instead of someone I love and therefore need to protect from my grief.

He nods, watching me as I wipe my eyes.

'Her heart just stopped beating one day. I should have known; I should have noticed. She'd stopped moving, but by the time I realised, it was too late. I had to go into the hospital, go through labour, knowing that she was dead. A stillbirth they call it. Which sounds so peaceful, you know? But it's not peaceful at all. Until afterwards, when there should be a cry and new life. But there's nothing; only silence. A terrible, empty silence... And then I finally held her in my arms, no breath, not moving, but so perfect...' I pause, overwhelmed by another gust of grief. 'And just now, the song... the littlest child, dreaming it was in paradise. I hope that's where she is. But I don't really believe in that stuff, you know.' I hiccup with another sob. 'Sorry. I shouldn't be saying all this to you.'

I have no idea whether the priest understands what I'm telling him, but he sits there quietly, listening. And maybe even if he doesn't understand all the words, he sees my sorrow and my pain. Maybe he understands that it's hard for me to say all of this, but that I need to say it to someone, finally, so he sits on and lets me talk.

When I finish, he's quiet for a moment. Then asks, 'What was her name?'

I look at him blankly.

'Your baby daughter, what did you call her?'

People don't usually ask that question. Perhaps they assume we never named her. Or maybe it's just easier not to know, not to think of her as a real person.

I look down at the crumpled handkerchief, which I've twisted into a ball. And I whisper, 'Lucie. We called her Lucie.'

My voice cracks as I say the name. A name I haven't said aloud for so long. And it feels just a tiny bit better, as if some of the pressure in my heart has eased a little, with being able to say these things out loud at long last.

I turn and smile at him through my tears. 'Spelt the French way, after my *Mamie* Lucie.'

He nods. And sits a while longer.

Then he says, 'It means "light" you know. From the Latin. If you wanted, you could light a candle to Saint Nicolas today. I know you don't believe in these things,' and he smiles serenely as I demur, embarrassed, realising that he has clearly understood everything I've said, 'but sometimes a simple, practical gesture of remembrance can be a balm for the soul when we are grieving. Lucie. Let her light shine in the darkness. I always think that that is the essence of the Christmas season: making the light shine out through the darkest time of the year, *n'est-ce pas?'*

After he's gone, I stay a while longer. I feel utterly drained—all that crying, I suppose—and yet I feel a sense of relief too. As if I've set down a heavy load that I've been carrying all alone, for so very long.

The wooden pew is polished and worn with use and I think of the many people who have sat here before me, full of hope and fear, joy and grief, for christenings and weddings and funerals. And suddenly I feel the cocoon of loneliness that has been my straitjacket for the past year fall away. How strange it is to feel so comforted here, amongst strangers in a foreign land. But I realise that I needed to come away from all that was familiar to be able to regain my perspective. To begin the painful process of letting go of the dead and to start to rebuild my life again.

Taking the priest's advice, I drop a coin in the box and take a candle. I hold the wick to the flame of another of the slender wax tapers—someone else's bright-burning gesture of sadness or gladness—and then set it into the holder. For Lucie. The flame burns steadily, unwavering, like my love for her. 'Look after her for me, Saint Nicolas,' I whisper.

Emerging into the marketplace again, I stand and blink. The fog has burned away completely and the church steeple now soars into a dizzying blue sky overhead. Bright winter sunlight dazzles my eyes and I set down my shopping basket for a moment to delve in my purse for my sunglasses.

The world looks newly made.

I take a deep breath.

And then step out into it.

Chapter 4

Les Anges dans nos campagnes

Angels in the countryside...

I drive home through a landscape that looks completely altered in the winter sunshine. Instead of sombre tones of brown and black, muffled by the pale mist, the countryside is suddenly a technicolour palette of lush green and rich russet, studded here and there with garnet-red berries. And instead of a dull, gunmetal grey, the sky is a broad sheet of blue. I feel quite light-headed as I drive up the hill and turn in at the little white sign to Les Pélerins.

I stow away my purchases in the refrigerator and then sit down to a plate of bread and cheese for lunch. I don't seem to have the appetite for anything more substantial, despite my earlier resolution to cook a proper meal. I promise myself I'll do better this evening.

At first, I put the fact that my head aches and my legs feel heavy and stiff down to all that emotion in the church. No wonder I feel light-headed; it was the first moment of real peace I've felt in a year. Leaving my plate of food half-eaten, I rest my throbbing forehead on my hands. And suddenly realise that I'm really not very well at all. My fingers are cold against the burning skin of my face and the stiffness in my legs seems to have spread into my back and neck. And—oh no!—I feel sick to my stomach...

I drag myself through to the sitting room, collapse onto the sofa and begin to shiver with fever. I should light the fire, but I'm too tired to bring in a basket of logs from the wood store. I've run out of kindling too, and the thought of going out to chop some more, or to gather some dry sticks from beneath the oaks, is too much to contemplate. I curl into a ball, pull a woollen throw over myself and lie there, alternately freezing and burning. Feeling, I now realise, really, *really* sick. And utterly wretched. I think, *no one knows. I can't call anyone. What if I seriously need help?*

And then I close my eyes, which feel oh so heavy, and drift into oblivion...

I don't know how long I've slept, but the soft violet glow of dusk hangs over the hillside and the first lights are coming on in the valley below when a pounding in my head awakens me.

I lie there, my limbs so heavy that I can't even lift my hand to check the time on my watch. And then I hear it again, a persistent knocking sound, which seems to be coming from somewhere outside my head now, but I can't quite make out where. My lips are dry and there's an unpleasant metallic taste on my tongue. My skin is burning up and yet I feel frozen to my very core with a chill that makes my bones ache.

The knocking falls silent for a few moments and then resumes again, a bit louder this time. *Front door*, I think. It takes every ounce of willpower I have to heave my legs over the edge of the sofa and pull myself upright. As I do so, my head spins and my stomach churns. Squinting through the blinding agony of a headache that makes my vision blur and weave, I creep to the hallway, holding on to the walls to steady myself.

I open the door. And blink.

Because there in the dusk, just turning to leave, is Bradley Cooper himself.

Confused, and hazy with fever, I stand and stare, realising that I've truly gone and done it now; I really shouldn't have watched The Playbook so often and I really shouldn't have let myself retreat into my parallel life so much. It's official: I've totally flipped.

And I'm even more certain that I'm hallucinating when he smiles his utterly gorgeous smile and says, in a low voice with a fabulously sexy French accent, '*Bonsoir*. I am so sorry to disturb you, *Madame*. But I wonder if you perhaps 'ave a grater I could borrow? You see, I 'ave a truffle and I wish to make a delicious omelette. But, alas, I 'ave no grater...'

Oh, my God, this has to be the best hallucination ever!

It's a pity I feel so terrible because otherwise I would definitely try to keep it going longer. But— maybe it's the mention of the truffle omelette—my fever-wracked body rebels suddenly.

I lean forward and throw up, all over Bradley Cooper's shoes.

They're black leather brogues, I notice in a detached kind of a way, the sort that have a pattern of little holes punched into them. They're going to be hell to clean.

The smile on Bradley's face fades to an expression of concern. He takes hold of my arm, with a grip that's surprisingly strong for a hallucination, and touches the fingertips of his other hand to my forehead.

'Oh!' I say, because it feels so nice to have a cool, capable hand press against my fevered brow (especially Bradley's hand)! And because I don't seem to be capable of saying anything else.

'*Madame*, you are unwell. We must get you into bed.'

I groan. Not just because I feel so bad, but also because this is such a horrible waste. Bradley Cooper is proposing to get me into bed and I'm too sick to do anything about it. He props me against the door-frame and then, gingerly, slips off his be-spattered shoes, stepping into the hallway in his stocking feet.

'Where is the bedroom?'

My tongue appears to be swollen and sticky and I can only mumble indistinctly, swaying with a dizziness that makes me nearly black out.

He cranes his head, looking past me to the open door of the sitting room. 'Okay, come. Let us get you in here.'

He guides me through and helps me onto the sofa. I draw my knees up to my chest again, shivering violently, as he arranges the woollen throw over me.

I hear his footsteps cross back to the front door and then leave, crunching away across the gravel. 'Don't go, Bradley!' I try to call after him, but all that comes out is a weak croak.

Damn! That'll teach me to throw up in the middle of the best dream ever.

I let my impossibly heavy eyelids close again, and sleep pulls me under...

There's a light now; one of the lamps on the console table has been switched on. And there's a soft pillow under my head instead of the rough fabric of the sofa. I open my eyes a tad, squinting against the light.

The best news of all is that Bradley is back! He crosses the room and shakes my arm gently. '*Madame*, you need to take these. Here, some water to wash them down.'

I prop myself onto one elbow and take the pills he's offering me, gulping down the water which cools the acid-seared soreness in my throat.

'That's good. Drink it all if you can.'

I collapse back onto the pillow and open my eyes a little wider. There he stands, gazing down at me: dark, wavy hair pushed back from his brow; a shadow of stubble emphasising the chiselled V of his jawline; and those gorgeous blue eyes, the colour of a clear winter sky.

Perhaps I've died and gone to heaven. *Please, God, let this moment last forever*, I think.

'Okay, you'll feel a little better soon. The fever should begin to come down a bit now. And if you think you're going to vomit again, I've put a bucket here beside you.'

Hmm, well that certainly spoiled the magic of the moment. A pretty practical dude, old Bradley.

Although...

Perhaps it's the distinctly un-romantic mention of the bucket that does it, or perhaps those pills are getting to work fast, but my mind begins to clear a little and so does my vision. I manage a weak smile of remorse and regret.

'Thank you,' I whisper to Bradley Cooper's French lookalike.

'*Je vous en prie,*' he replies, his face creasing into a broad smile of relief—probably because I'm not looking like throwing up again anytime soon. 'Apologies; we haven't been properly introduced. I'm your neighbour, Didier Dumas.'

I'm befuddled and confused with fever, so it takes a moment for this to sink in. 'But I thought my neighbour was Doctor Lebrun?'

He shakes his head. '*Docteur* Lebrun has retired. He and his wife have gone to La Réunion for the winter. I am *Docteur* Dumas, a locum. I'm standing in for him until a replacement can be found.'

I digest all of this for a few moments. Then, with an effort, gather my wits about me. 'Evie Brooke. I'm a friend of Rose and Max's, the owners of this house. And I'm *so* sorry. This is the most terrible way to have introduced myself. I don't know what came over me, but whatever it was, it was nasty and it was sudden!'

'The norovirus, I expect. A winter vomiting bug. It does the rounds at this time of year. Perhaps you picked it up on your journey down here. You seem to have a very violent strain of it, but don't worry,' he stops and presses his cool fingertips into the sides and back of my neck, 'it doesn't look like anything more serious. I've given you paracetamol and something to help settle the nausea. And now you must drink lots of fluids because you were dangerously dehydrated with the fever and the vomiting.'

I do wish he'd stop reminding me about the vomiting. Partly because it makes my stomach churn again; and partly because it's excruciatingly embarrassing remembering what I did to his nice shiny shoes by way of saying hello.

I close my eyes again. It's comforting to lie there, the shivering slowly subsiding, my body beginning to relax, and listen to the sounds of someone else moving about the room. It reminds me of being at home with Will, the two of us so comfortable together that we took each other's presence for granted. I remember the soundtrack of our everyday lives, back in the days before grief silenced us: the sound of him clattering down the stairs, whistling cheerfully; the hammering and drilling as he put up shelves, just after we moved in, while I painted the room next door, both of us singing along to the radio that blared from the hallway; the quiet thud of the refrigerator door closing as he pushed it to with his elbow, his arms full of ingredients for the meal we'd be making together; working alongside one another in the kitchen, chopping and mixing and stirring. 'Here Evie, taste this and tell me what you think,' he'd say, as we experimented with new dishes for the bistro before opening day...

I've gotten used to being on my own, and it's only now that I realise how much I've missed the company of others. Or *an* other.

I open my eyes a fraction and watch Dishy Doctor Didier from under my eyelashes as he brings in kindling and makes a fire. It feels totally unreal, lying here uselessly like this while a complete stranger looks after me but, sick as I am, there's nothing else I can do. His footsteps approach and I quickly shut my eyes, feigning sleep. He comes to kneel beside the sofa and gently pats my shoulder to rouse me.

'There, now we will get some warmth into the house,' he smiles. I may feel like death warmed up, and he may have a wife or girlfriend waiting for him back at home for all I know, but even so my heart rate picks up a little at the sight of those beautiful blue eyes so close to mine.

'*Merci*,' I croak.

'And now, *Madame* Brooke, you must get into bed and I will bring you a glass of this delicious electrolyte powder'—he waves a sachet at me—'which you must try to sip. And then I will leave you to sleep, which is the best medicine of all.'

He helps me up and I manage to climb the stairs, brush my teeth and splash some cold water on my face. I put on a pair of warm flannel pyjamas, the functioning part of my brain wishing that I'd packed some rather more alluring nightwear; they're not exactly Victoria's most titillating Secret. But then the last thing I had expected was that I'd be entertaining Bradley Cooper's equally gorgeous French cousin in them.

He knocks on the bedroom door and sets a glass of the rehydration drink down on the bedside cabinet. 'I have also taken the precaution of bringing you the bucket, in case of further vomiting.'

Seriously, is he *never* going to let the vomiting thing drop?

He looks around the room, taking in the simple furnishings, which are perfect for a summer holiday home but look a little spartan in the winter.

'You have no heating in here? Wait there!'

ATER 4   87

Wait there? Listen Didier, *mon ami*, I'm going nowhere. Firstly, because I have nowhere else to go; secondly, because I feel so lousy right now that I don't think I'd be capable of moving even if I wanted to; and thirdly because you are gorgeous.

... I hope I said that in my head and not out loud by mistake; too much time living alone will do that to you.

I'm beginning to feel drowsy again and let my eyes close, so thankful to be resting my aching bones here in my comfortable bed.

He creeps into the room with an electric radiator which he plugs in. It ticks quietly to itself, warming up and radiating a gentle heat into the chill air of the bedroom.

'Try to drink all of that if you can. And I'm leaving these'—he shows me a blister pack of paracetamol—'right here, so you can take two more if you wake up in the night. There's a jug of water too, you see? I'm going to leave your front door on the latch and I'll look in on you in the morning. But these bugs are usually a short, sharp shock. Twenty-four hours and the vomiting should stop.'

Okay, *puh-lease*, that's it; we're done with the mentioning of the vomiting already!

'I'm just next door. Come and get me if you start to feel worse again.'

I nod, obediently take a sip from the glass and then settle my aching head on the pillow.

'*Bonne nuit, Madame* Brooke,' he says softly. And I drift into a deep sleep and dream that I'm dancing with Bradley Cooper in a church lit by a thousand candles, until Will appears and tips a bucket of water (thankfully nothing worse!) over both our heads.

◆ ◆ ◆

When you're trying to become a hermit and shut yourself off from the rest of the world, being pole-axed by a winter bug turns out to be an excellent way of getting to know your neighbours.

I woke on Sunday morning, weak as a rag doll, but no longer running the raging temperature, and managed to get showered and dressed, stagger downstairs to refill the pitcher of water and then collapse onto the sofa. Didier must have banked up the fire before he left the previous night, because there were still enough glowing embers to coax it back into life. So, by the time he came to check on me, I was lying under the woollen throw, before the cheerful blaze in the hearth, gazing at the glorious day outside the window.

A crisp frost, like the fine dusting of icing sugar on a chocolate torte, covered the ground; the apple tree's rosy baubles, bright as the colours in a child's painting, were outlined against the backcloth of perfect blue and, as I lay watching, the robin hopped and fluttered between the branches and the frozen earth beneath. It's very beautiful, my Not-Christmas tree.

There was a knock at the door and then Didier called, 'Hello? It's only me.'

I heaved myself a little more upright and smoothed my hair behind my ears. 'I'm in here.'

'*Bonjour, Madame* Brooke. It's good to see you looking a little better this morning. How are you feeling?'

'Please, call me Evie. I've stopped wishing I could curl up and die, thanks. So a lot better than last night.'

He checked my temperature. 'Still above normal, but it's come down a few degrees. The worst should be over now. Have you been able to keep the fluids down?'

I nodded. 'Yes, as you can see I'm living dangerously without the bucket this morning. But don't worry; I think it's now safe to stand within a yard of me.'

He smiled. Well, one thing was for sure, I hadn't hallucinated those blue eyes yesterday. And, even in the clear light of day and without a raging fever, he still did bear an uncanny resemblance to Bradley Cooper.

'What do you feel like for breakfast? Do you think you could manage a little dry toast?'

I shook my head firmly as my stomach did a somersault at the mention of anything more substantial than water.

'Just some rehydration drink then. Take it slowly. Lots of water and rest today, okay? Don't go doing anything too energetic like, say, chasing pigs for example!'

But of course. Mortification dawned as I realised that my gorgeous Bradley-lookalike neighbour must have enjoyed every moment of my less-than-graceful frolicking on the terrace the previous morning. Ah well, at least I could blame my flaming cheeks on my high temperature rather than my confusion... But I was still feeling too sick to care very much for very long.

The last thing I heard was Didier bringing in another basket of logs and building up the fire. Suddenly exhausted again, I rested my head back onto the pillow, drowsy in the warmth of the sunlit room, and drifted off to sleep.

And now it's Monday morning and I'm feeling like a new woman. Albeit one with a slightly dizzy head and wobbly legs, but the headache and nausea have passed, thank the Lord. I fill the kettle and, as it begins to hum to itself, I try to slice a little of the bread—now hard and stale—from the market on Saturday. It was only the day before yesterday, but it seems an age ago that I was sitting in the church listening to the children sing the song of Saint Nicolas.

The *baguette* looks too unappetising even for toast. Gingerly, in case it proves too much for my still-delicate constitution, I unwrap the basket of cookies and nibble on the corner of one of the frosted stars. In fact the sweet gingerbread seems, if anything, to settle my stomach—and it's certainly a lot more appetising than the electrolyte sachets that Didier's left me—so I retire to the sofa and lie in front of the cheerfully blazing fire with a mug of weak tea and another of the cookies. How wonderful it is to feel well again, or at least so much better.

I wonder whether Didier will call in today. Of course he'll be working as it's a weekday. But it would be nice to thank him properly for his help and his kindness. And, if I'm honest, to have a chance to get to know him better. Now that my head is no longer a confusion of fever-induced dreams, certain questions come to mind. Such as, is he (a) married or (b) gay?

Those seem to be the two most likely options for a guy that good-looking.

And, as I sip my tea and savour the softly spiced cookie, which is almost as therapeutic as a hug from my *Mamie* Lucie, I realise that I may just be getting better in more ways than one.

So, I muse, the recipe for curing grief turns out to be as follows: take equal measures of sadness and pain; mix together with some words of comfort, the kindness of strangers and some memories of happier times; bake at a high temperature for some length of time; then allow to rest, until well-risen and lighter than before.

'*Coucou!*' My train of thought is interrupted by the arrival of a visitor, but it's not Doctor Didier.

'*Entrez!*' I call, and in walks a tall, elderly lady whose pure white hair is tied back in an elegant chignon. She wears work clothes, corduroy pants and a thick sweater, and her hands, which are holding a heavy-looking cast-iron casserole, are work-roughened, the bare nails cut short.

'*Oh, pardonnez-moi, Madame*, I wasn't sure whether you'd be out of bed. Didier said the door was unlocked. He asked me to check on you this morning. I'll just put this in the kitchen, if I may?'

I scramble to my feet and come to show her the way, even though it's clear she knows the layout of the house well. She sets the casserole down and then proffers a hand. 'Eliane Dubosq. Pleased to meet you at last, *Madame* Brooke.'

'Please, call me Evie. I'm so delighted you've come. And I'm sorry I haven't thanked you for your lovely Saint Nicolas Day gift—I assume it was from you— but events rather overtook me.'

'I know,' she smiles and nods. 'Didier told me. No need to apologise. And it's good that you are back on your feet again now. I've brought you some soup, made with vegetables from my garden. You will need to regain your strength.'

'Please, will you have a cup of tea? And I can offer you one of these delicious cookies, which were clearly baked by an expert!'

We settle down in the sitting room and she gazes about her. 'It's nice to have the house lived in at this time of year for a change. Usually it's sad and cold here in the winter. I like looking out of my window and seeing the smoke from the chimneys of both the houses over on this side of the road, seeing signs of life. When I heard Anne and Gilles Lebrun were off to La Réunion, I thought Mathieu and I were going to have a very lonely winter indeed at Les Pélerins—the last ones left! Having you two young people here is a sign that there's still hope for the countryside. Most people want to live in cities nowadays.'

She shakes her head sorrowfully. 'The rural way of life seems to be dying out, just at a time when the world needs it more than ever.'

I nod. 'My grandmother always used to say we should live our lives with the seasons. I guess in the city, people are less tuned in to that rhythm. It's easy to become disconnected from it.'

'Precisely. When we begin to take Mother Nature for granted, it's no wonder she gets angry and takes her revenge on us with all this strange weather. She is a woman, after all, and we women don't take kindly to being ignored!'

It's another beautiful day today, so it's easy to forget the leaden skies and the dense fog of a day or two ago but, now she comes to mention it, the weather has been pretty changeable.

'Is this more typical?' I ask her. 'This lovely sunshine?'

'*Oui*, but don't take it for granted. There are thirteen moons this year, so we can expect things to be pretty turbulent.'

'Thirteen moons? What does that mean?'

'Every now and then we get a year that has thirteen full moons. Check your diary, if it shows the phases, and you'll see. And folklore tells us that, in years which have thirteen moons, we can expect storms. In all ways. It's not just confined to the weather. Our individual lives, world events, war, flood, famine; thirteen moons mean trouble. Of course,' she smiles, 'it's only folklore. But if we pause in our busy lives for a moment and ponder where that folklore comes from, we find it's usually based on some foundation of truth. Those of us who live in the countryside like to mix our science with a good pinch of superstition too, you see.'

She pauses to take a sip of her tea.

'Now, tell me, Evie, how are you settling in? Rose told us that you were in need of a refuge and that you were seeking peace and quiet. That's why I didn't come straight round when you arrived; I wanted to give you some space. Are you all right here? Not too lonely?' Her direct French way of asking is refreshing after so many months of politely tactful British skirting around the issue.

'I'm fine. Although I was just starting to miss conversation and human company when I got sick. It's a great way to meet the neighbours, I've discovered! Although I'm not sure I made the best impression on poor Didier. I really wasn't very nice to know when we met.'

'Don't you worry; he's used to it in his line of work.' Eliane pats my hand reassuringly.

'How long has he been here?' I ask, hopefully nonchalantly enough to disguise any whiff of a vested interest.

She shoots me a keen glance though and I know I'm not pulling any wool over those clear grey eyes that seem able to read my innermost thoughts.

'He took over from Doctor Lebrun when he retired in September. Didier came to us from Paris—another escapee to the country. So the easiest thing was for him to move into Anne and Gilles' house while things are in a state of flux. We all wish he'd stay, but he says it's just temporary until the commune can find a permanent replacement. It's not so easy these days though, finding people who want to come and live the rural life.'

She shoots me another appraising glance. 'Rose tells me you are a cook. And a very talented one, at that.'

'Rose is a very dear friend and therefore totally biased. But yes, I love cooking. Or did love it. I've kind of lost my way of late...' I trail off, unsure of how much Rose has said to Eliane. She nods encouragingly, those wise, grey eyes warm with compassion.

'But, you know,' I continue, 'when I went to the market on Saturday I felt inspired again. All that wonderful produce, so fresh, and so many delicious ingredients. I'm tempted to start again, just as soon as I've got my strength back.'

'Good,' she nods approvingly. 'Such a talent should not go to waste. When you feel strong enough, come and visit me. I'll show you my garden and give you some of the freshest vegetables this rich earth can produce. And in the meantime,' she stands up, getting ready to take her leave, 'get some rest and then eat some of that good soup for lunch. You'll soon be back on your feet.'

After saying goodbye, I wander back into the kitchen and lift the lid of the casserole. The soup smells tempting, even to my still somewhat jaded palate: a clear chicken broth chock-full of carrots, leeks and potatoes. Just the kind my grandmother used to make, I think. And that thought prompts another. Losing Lucie made me lose my appetite. Not only my physical appetite for food, but my appetite for cooking, which used to be my consuming passion. Without Will, without the bistro, my channel for expressing my love of life—nourishing my own body and soul by nourishing others—had gone. And ever since then I've been starving. This simple pot of soup represents more than just the thoughtful gesture of a kind neighbour: it's a sign, pointing the way out of the dark tunnel I've been lost in for so long. Soul food.

Mamie Lucie's notebook catches my eye. The pages are dog-eared with use and the card feels soft beneath my fingers as I open the cover. Written inside, in her neat, cursive script, is my grandmother's name. And beneath it, the handwriting a little shakier by then, she'd written my name. I'd forgotten that, even though I used to use the notebook almost every day. Did it help her to know, when her own days were drawing to an end, that she would live on through her recipes, trusting me to keep her love alive even after she'd gone? I feel ashamed suddenly, as if I've let her down. I glance again at Eliane's casserole of *potage*. Like the St Nicolas Day cookies, the food seems to be a message, a gentle nudge of encouragement from *Mamie*. Inspired, I pick up the notebook and retreat with it to curl up before the fire and trawl for recipes that make use of the best winter produce.

An hour later, I've picked out several recipes that I'm going to try, searching out the ingredients in the local stores and markets, maybe adapting and improving the dishes as I go along, giving them an updated twist. And I've even gone so far as to draft a Christmas lunch menu (even though, obviously, there isn't going to be a Christmas lunch this year), as follows:

Glass of champagne with gruyere gougères

◆

Six oysters (Marennes number 3?)

◆

Fillet of sea bream with a winter salad of chicory, lamb's lettuce and walnuts

◆

Duck breast with a red wine jus, dauphinoise potatoes, roasted root vegetables with rosemary and thyme

◆

Cheeseboard

◆

Caramelised clementines with sabayon

I look at my handiwork and sigh. It's not really the same, cooking a meal like that when you have no one to share it with. For a moment I imagine inviting Didier to come over and enjoy a Christmas feast with me. Perhaps we'd end up in front of the fire with another glass of the champagne...

I sigh again, chiding myself. He'll obviously have some place to be on Christmas Day, a guy like that. Family; a wife; a girlfriend at the very least. Setting my notes and *Mamie* Lucie's recipe book aside, I go and heat up a bowl of Eliane's soup and settle down to a solitary lunch. Perhaps, more realistically, my Christmas menu should read:

Bowl of soup

♦

Bread and cheese

♦

An apple

After all, it is just going to be a day like any other.

Outside my window, the robin flutters to the very top of the apple tree and flaunts its bright breast, catching my eye. My Not-Christmas tree really does look very pretty in the dazzle of the low-lying December sun. I remember Eliane's warning about the thirteen moons. There's not a cloud in the sky, not a breath of wind.

Seriously, what a lot of nonsense these superstitions are!

Chapter 5
I Wonder as I Wander

I wonder as I wander out under the sky...

The beautiful weather continues, day in, day out, the temperature plummeting overnight under clear, star-filled skies so that each morning I wake to a crisp frost. But where the sun's long fingers brush the ground, the whiteness is soon erased and the vivid greens and rich russet browns reappear, as if by magic.

I wouldn't say the nights have gotten any more peaceful though. My sleeping hours are sandwiched between the muffled thumping and clattering sounds from the garage (what *does* Didier get up to in there when he gets home from work every day?), the alarming screech of the owl as it launches itself out of the horse barn (I caught a glimpse of it one night, a ghost-like apparition with wide white wings outstretched), and the triumphant crowing of the rooster as he announces the pre-dawn arrival of another perfect day. But in between these disturbances, there's a silence so profound that my sleep is deep and dreamless, with no need for the assistance of sleeping pills, my body a glutton for rest as I recover from my illness.

And maybe, just maybe, I'm beginning to recover from the shock and pain of losing Lucie. It's coming up to the one-year anniversary, but instead of the bleak dread that I'd anticipated, a glimmer of acceptance seems to flicker in the darkness of my mind, exactly the way the candle's tiny flame burned bravely in the half-light of the church. I've resolved that I'll buy a single, beautiful candle and light it on Christmas Eve, letting it shine out into the darkness just like the priest said. A candle of remembrance. And maybe, just maybe, a candle of hope as well.

How strange it is that I fled here to the peace and quiet of the countryside (ha!) to try and escape my grief, and yet I seem to have found myself coming face to face with it in a way that I never did in London. The kindness of strangers has helped me begin to rebuild my strength, I guess. And, while I was hoping to find a cure for my grief—for which there can be no cure—I'm starting to realise that perhaps time and the gentle, unobtrusive support of this tiny community are helping me at least accept my loss; helping the scars to begin to heal so that, whilst they'll still always be there, life will go on.

Today I've got enough strength back to follow the pilgrim path up the road to the crest of the hill and see if I can get a signal on my phone up there. I need to catch up with my family and with Rose too, before they send out a search party to make sure I'm still alive. I guess Rose would have called Eliane again if she'd been really anxious about me though.

I step out of the door and into the sunlight, zipping up my fleece jacket. And nearly jump out of my skin. Because, ambling round the corner of the horse barn, here comes that pig again, squinting at me with its little pink-rimmed eyes and wrinkling up its fleshy snout as it catches my scent. It's huge; a vast, flesh-coloured beast tottering along on its tiny trotters.

'Shoo!' I say, not very convincingly. *Do pigs bite?* I wonder. It grunts, unimpressed, and saunters non-chalantly on past me, disappearing round the corner of the house in search of more windfall apples. For a moment I contemplate going to try and chase it away again (carefully making sure first that no one's watching from the windows of the doctor's house this time). But actually I'm quite grateful to it for making me laugh at myself the other day, jolting me out of my misery with its disdain for my city ways. And anyway, I figure it's probably safer there in the garden than roaming the country lanes, so I set off, planning to call in at Eliane's house on my way past.

As I cross the road, a shaggy black dog bounces up to the fence alongside Eliane and Mathieu's cottage, and barks at me. Eliane appears in the doorway, wiping her hands on the apron she's wearing.

'Quiet, Bruno! Sorry, Evie, he's just announcing your arrival.' She pats his broad head and he wags his tail, approvingly. 'How are you feeling?'

'Much better, thanks. Your soup was delicious. I'm just going up the hill to see if I can get in touch with the outside world.' I produce the phone from my pocket. 'It's a beautiful day.'

She shakes her head, looking doubtful. 'It's fine at the moment, but it'll be the thirteenth full moon in another week and then we'll see changes. Mark my words, this won't last!'

I give her a cheery wave and set off again. 'Oh, and by the way,' I call, turning back, 'there's a very large pig on my front lawn. He's come to raid the apple tree. Does he belong to you?'

'*Zut!* That animal is a veritable Houdini. Mathieu!' she calls into the house behind her. 'The pig's escaped again!' She turns back to me. 'Sorry. He probably knows his time is nearly up. He keeps making bids for freedom, but fortunately he only gets as far as your apples and then gets distracted. We'll be butchering him next week. Would you perhaps like to come and help? I could do with an extra pair of hands when it comes to making the pâtés and sausages.'

'Er, okay,' I say cautiously. I'm not sure *like* is quite the right word. But it'll certainly be a new experience. I feel a little squeamish at the thought of the poor pig, that I now feel I know personally, meeting its end, but then I can't really call myself a chef if I'm not prepared to see the whole process through from beginning to end. 'Let me know when.'

I continue up the hill, following the cockleshell way-markers in the footsteps of a thousand pilgrims, soon getting out of breath as the road begins to rise more steeply, my weakened legs aching with the climb. In the ditch that runs alongside the country lane, a little stream babbles busily on its way down to join the river in the valley below. I pause for a rest and gaze back towards the cluster of buildings I've left behind. It looks like a toy farm. The white horse is grazing peacefully in the field on this side of the house. And I can make out Mathieu gently coaxing the pig back up to its enclosure with a tin bucket of feed.

I'm overheating now with the effort of the climb, so I take off my fleece jacket and tie the sleeves around my waist, turning to trudge onwards and upwards. Eventually I reach the top and pause, hands on hips, to take in the view. The cluster of buildings at Les Pélerins looks even more toy-like from up here, and I can see the château above Eliane and Mathieu's house, which is hidden in the cedars and pines that surround it when viewed from below. Very faintly in the distance a church clock tolls the hour. Up here, the land falls away on all sides, undulating gently, and there are rows and rows and then more rows of vines as far as the eye can see. Far off, a tractor ploughs a fresh furrow. And way down at the bottom of the valley, the Dordogne River meanders across its wide plain. Above me, its wings beating against the sky, a bird of prey hovers, its body suspended, perfectly still between the rapid flicker of its wing feathers. Disturbed by my presence, perhaps, it swoops away across the vineyard in search of happier hunting elsewhere.

Suddenly the phone in my pocket begins to beep as it picks up a signal and messages flood in. I spread my jacket on the ground in front of an old milestone; *Sainte-Foy-La-Grande 6 km* is chiselled into it. I settle down, leaning my back against its lichen-encrusted face; in this weather, it's not a bad place to make my office.

First I deal with the backlog of emails. There are several from my mother, briskly cheerful, describing the pre-Christmas fundraiser she's organising; and Rose has sent me several jokes and a couple of chatty messages. I reply to Rose, briefly telling her about my illness and the fortuitous turnover of doctors at Les Pélerins since her last visit. Then I check a weather forecast for the coming week. As Eliane said, it shows the moon waxing until it reaches a full circle in a week's time, so she was right about that, even if she was wrong about the weather that accompanies it, which looks like it's going to be unremittingly sunny, with no wind to speak of and the now-familiar pattern of cold nights and warmer days. So much for the folklore then.

I hesitate for a moment, leaning back against the solid stone behind me and tipping my face upwards to allow the gentle rays of December sunshine to soak into my pale cheeks. Then, before I can over-think it, I log in to Facebook and look up my sister Tess's page. I click '*like*' beneath a photo of her that a friend's uploaded, looking radiant, the curve of her belly showing clearly now. And I write '*Greetings from sunny France! You BOTH look beautiful. XXX*'

I breathe out a long, slow breath and close my eyes for a few moments, savouring the feeling of relief that flows through my veins. It's a start, a thawing of the silence that's sat between us these past few months, heavy and unmoveable. I know she'll understand.

It's been another of the desperately sad things I've had to bear, the sudden awkwardness in my relationship with my beloved sister, the ripples of the fallout from losing Lucie expanding outwards and engulfing more than just my marriage, fracturing other bonds. So much has gone unsaid between Tess and me, where before there was an unbroken—and, we thought, unbreakable—flow of communication between us.

I gaze out at the view before me, the sunlight making the river sparkle like a strand of golden tinsel draped festively across the December landscape.

I know that, on top of everything else, I've been failing in my duty to support my little sister. I should have been rejoicing with her every day of her pregnancy, instead of blighting it with my sorrow. Seeing that photo of her seven-month bump—even though I did feel a pang of pain—has made me realise that soon I will have a niece or nephew to cuddle and play with and love to bits; and so the pain is mixed with a wave of joy as well. Such conflicting emotions. But, I realise, feeling them is better, by far, than the dull numbness that's gone before.

My phone rings suddenly and I jump at the sound, unaccustomed to it after all these days of radio silence. It's Rose. I smile as her voice squawks in my ear, demanding to hear the low-down on the dishy new neighbour, and we chat for a good half hour, catching up with each other's news.

My feet and my heart feel lighter as I head back down the hill afterwards.

With renewed energy, I re-fill the log basket and stoke the fire against the early evening chill. I've run out of kindling again, so I decide it's time to take the bull by the horns—or, rather, the axe by the handle— and chop some more. Up until now I've gotten by on what Didier brought in and, when that ran out, some dry sticks gleaned from underneath the oak trees. But now it's time to channel my inner lumberjack and get to grips with a proper supply of neatly chopped kindling. It's not something I've done for years, since I used to help Dad split sticks up at the lake house. But how hard can it be?

There's a hatchet sticking into the edge of a large slab of tree trunk that serves as a chopping block. I lever it out, running a finger gingerly along its sharp blade. Okay, we just balance a log on here, like so, and take a swing... I hit the edge of the log a glancing blow and it falls to the ground. Try again. Only this time I guess I need to hold it in place with my other hand. I raise the hatchet and swing again...

Unfortunately, at that very moment, Didier's car sweeps into the yard, disturbing my concentration. So he's just in time to see me slice my left index finger with the axe, dropping the log as the blood starts to flow copiously from my hand.

I'm not sure what hurts more: my hand or my pride.

He ushers me into his house and sits me down on a kitchen chair, wrapping several sheets of paper towel tightly round my finger and making me hold it above my head.

'*Oh,* là-là, Evie, it's a good job you live next door to a doctor! How on earth did you manage to survive back in London?'

I blush furiously, annoyed with myself for appearing such a klutz, as he cleans the wound and expertly pulls the edges of the deep cut together with butterfly strips. He puts a neat dressing over it and then steps back to survey his handiwork.

'I think perhaps I should cut kindling for you from now on,' he smiles.

'I'm perfectly capable, thank you...' I start to object, but he shakes his head.

'It's no trouble; I'll just do a few extra sticks when I'm cutting my own supply. Please—otherwise I won't be able to go out and treat my other patients if I have to stay here watching over you the whole time.'

Humph, what a nerve! I'm sure I can manage; I just need a little more practice. My finger throbs as a reminder of what happens when I *do* practice though. And his blue eyes really *do* crinkle in a way that makes it impossible to stay mad at his disparagement of my kindling-chopping skills for very long.

'Well, all right then,' I allow, grudgingly, 'but only if I can cook a meal for you in return?'

'Really? You cook?' His surprise isn't very flattering, but I guess I haven't exactly presented myself in the most practical of lights up to this point.

'Yes, I cook!' I retort, with a grin that matches his own teasing smile. 'You French don't have a total monopoly, you know. In fact, do I recall you saying something about a truffle the other day?'

He beams. '*Mais oui.* I never did get round to using it.'

'Okay, hand it over then. Tomorrow night, if you're free, I'll cook dinner for you.'

'It's a deal. I'll bring the wine. And the kindling too!'

I march back to my door carrying a paper bag in which a small, pungently scented Périgord truffle nestles, a little nugget of black gold. As I push the door open, I glance back across the yard. He's still standing in his doorway, watching me. I raise my hand with its clean white bandage. '*A demain.*'

And I'm thankful, as I duck back into my house, that he can't see the deep blush that floods my cheeks with colour once again.

◆ ◆ ◆

Didier sets down his knife and fork on the empty plate sitting on the table in front of him, and pushes back his chair, giving himself room to stretch out his long legs. '*Délicieux,*' he pronounces. 'Tell me again how you made that *purée;* it went so well with the fish.'

Having trawled *Mamie* Lucie's notebook and the local stores for inspiration, I'd made a creamy *purée* of cauliflower and laced it with a little truffle-infused oil, then laid fillets of sea bass on top and decorated the dish with a few wafer-thin shavings of earthy black truffle, which made an elegant contrast to the pale flesh of the fish. To add texture and colour, I fried little cakes of grated potato and carrot until they were crisp and golden.

'It's very simple; you just need a cauliflower and, of course, a truffle from a grateful patient. A little goes a long way, so there's still some of the truffle left over for you to take home and make your omelette tomorrow night. I'll let you in on a cook's secret too: if you put the truffle and the eggs all together in a paper bag for twenty-four hours, then the eggs will absorb the flavour and it'll be even more delicious.'

He raises one eyebrow, shooting me a quizzical glance. 'So tell me, how does an American who's come via England know some of the innermost secrets of French cooking?'

I smile. 'It's my inheritance from my French grandmother. She grew up in Périgord, near Sainte Alvère.'

'Ah, that explains your way with truffles then. Sainte Alvère is the very Mecca for gourmets. Do you know, they have a special Truffle Market there in the season? Every week, from December to February, people come from miles around to visit the *Marché aux Truffes*, where these inauspicious-looking fungi are bought and sold at about the same price, weight for weight, as gold. They end up in some of the world's finest restaurants. But I bet none of their dishes could beat that one.' He gestures with his wine glass towards his empty plate, which has been scraped clean.

'And now tell me, *Madame* Evie, what brings you to this little corner of the world at such a bleak time of the year?'

'It's hardly very bleak,' I laugh. 'This beautiful sunshine, day in, day out? I'm used to winters in London where it's grey and damp for months on end. And even those were a cake-walk compared to winters in Massachusetts; my dad's least favourite winter pastime is excavating the driveway from under yet another couple of feet of snow. Give me December in south-west France any day of the week.'

'Well, if you like it at this time of the year, you should try coming in the summertime! When I was a child, we used to spend our holidays down here. It's truly a paradise from spring through to autumn; first the trees come into blossom, then spring really gets going and there is a riot of colour everywhere: wisteria, lilacs, magnolias flowering in every garden and wildflowers spilling from the hedgerows. And then the first tender green leaves appear on those dead-looking sticks out there in the vineyard.' He waves his glass towards the window. 'In the autumn we have the wine harvest and then the vines turn to scarlet and gold; it's really a sight worth seeing. Thank goodness in the winter months we have this delicious liquid summer sunshine to keep us going!' He takes another sip of the Saint-Emilion that he's brought to accompany the meal. I'd hesitated when he handed me the bottle at the start of the evening: red wine with fish? But, in fact, it's gone perfectly with the robust flavours that the truffle has imparted to the food. I make a mental note to jot that down after he's gone, as a footnote to the recipe for future reference.

I place a platter of cheeses on the table between us and pour a little more of the wine into each of our glasses.

'So why *did* you come here?' Didier persists, not letting me off the hook with my attempts to divert the conversation with talk of the world's weather.

It's still hard to talk about Lucie. But I remind myself that, after all, it helped me begin to heal when I opened up to the priest that day in the church. I gather up my courage, pretending to concentrate on savouring a sliver of brie for a moment, contemplating the way the wine cuts through the richness of the cheese, giving myself time to choose my words carefully and keep my tone light.

Taking a deep breath, I say, 'I lost a baby. My marriage didn't survive. At least, my husband and I are separated, but I don't think there's going to be any way back. I got stuck; he moved on. Christmas is kind of a difficult time for me, so I thought I'd escape. And Max and Rose were kind enough to give me the loan of the house here as the perfect getaway.'

His blue eyes soften with compassion. My casual tone and forced smile clearly aren't fooling him. I drop my gaze, not wanting to let my emotions get the better of me. We hardly know each other, after all. Another fortifying sip of the wine helps.

'And how about you?' I ask, seizing the opportunity to divert the conversation away from my own predicament. 'You said you are only standing in until they find a replacement for Doctor Lebrun. So where did you come from originally?'

It's his turn to drop his gaze, and then those piercing, clear eyes meet mine again and I see there's a flicker of something darker beneath their smile. Like a shadow passing across the sun. He's silent for a few moments, and I sense he's also trying to pluck up his courage, struggling to find the right words for the answer to my question.

'I'm from Paris. And, like you, I'm on the run from Christmas. I was engaged to be married. Three years ago, my fiancée was driving up to Paris so that we could spend Christmas together. There was fog, a pile-up on the motorway. She was killed.'

We both sit, silent, for a moment, each digesting the other's words. And as we do, I sense something change between us, a new, unspoken understanding. In our different ways, we're both survivors of a terrible loss, struggling to come to terms with our grief, to find a way to start to live again. It feels as though the earth has shifted on its axis and suddenly there's a new gravitational force at play which bonds us to one another.

'I'm so sorry, Didier.' I reach out a hand to touch his. He lets it rest there for a moment, then folds his fingers over mine, giving my hand a squeeze.

'We have that in common then,' he smiles again. 'Someone to grieve for. Especially at this time of year.' He releases my hand and I cover my confusion with another sip from my glass.

Didier gazes out into the darkness beyond the terrace, the lights in the valley below mirroring the stars above that seem magnified by the frosty night air.

'I hate the fog,' he says, with feeling. 'I felt I was suffocating in it.' His voice becomes quieter, almost as if he's talking to himself... 'And then, like magic, it melted away and you appeared. With the sunshine in your hair. As if it was you who had driven the fog away.'

Our eyes meet again and we smile, understanding.

'Okay then, two *compadres*, united in our stand against Christmas!' I say. 'I tell you what, if you don't have a better offer, how about joining me for Not-Christmas lunch on the twenty-fifth? I've already started planning the menu.'

'After a meal such as this, how could a man possibly refuse? It's a date! Thank you, Evie, this has been wonderful. Perhaps, if I promise to bring you some more kindling for your fire, we could even consider doing this again. Before Not-Christmas?'

'With pleasure. I guess I still owe you for a couple of medical consultations too,' I smile ruefully, holding up my bandaged finger. 'This time next week, maybe?'

'That sounds perfect.' He pauses. 'Can I ask you one more thing? For Not-Christmas lunch? I've always wanted to try Christmas Pudding, since one of my English patients described it to me. It sounds such a bizarre idea, but they said it was delicious and traditional. Does an American know how to make such a thing? And is it possible to do so in France?'

I grin. 'I do love a culinary challenge! Of course I know how to make it, after living in Britain. I have the perfect recipe, as the result of a great deal of experimenting. Of course, it should really have been made about a month ago, and now be sitting steeped in brandy waiting for the big day. But I figure it won't matter too much. And if I can't find all the ingredients here then I can always improvise. One Not-Christmas Pudding coming right up!'

In bed that night, I lie awake mulling over the evening and our conversation. Each look; the touch of his fingers closing around mine; his smile.

In my head, I'm already starting to plan the menu for our next dinner together... And trying to work out how I can create a Franco-American traditional English Christmas Pudding in a fortnight.

A screech from outside, announcing the barn owl's nightly hunting trip, interrupts my train of thought. It's funny; it doesn't sound terrifying any more, but quite friendly really. Like it's just telling me it's there, acknowledging my presence here. *Happy hunting*, I think, and smile as I pull the covers up around me, going back to drawing up my mental list of pudding ingredients.

I guess I'll have something to report back to Rose on my next trip to the office at the top of the hill— and it looks as if I just might be getting my cooking mojo back again.

120

Chapter 6
The Boar's Head Carol

The boar's head in hand bear I,
Bedecked with bay and rosemary...

Mathieu is a huge, shaggy, bear of a man. He looks as if he'd be capable of wrestling a grizzly and coming out on top. He's also very, very shy. Whenever he sees me coming, he ducks his head and shambles off in the opposite direction, so all we've exchanged so far in the way of direct communication is a wave of the hand if he catches sight of me when he comes to bring the horse into the barn each evening. Eliane has told me they're taking particular care of the grey mare as she's in foal. Come spring, there should be a cute addition to the view from the windows of Rose's house.

So I'm surprised when, early one evening, there's a tentative tap at the door and I open it to find Mathieu standing there, blushing as pink as a boiled beet. In his hands, he wrings out the cloth cap which he's just whipped from his head, in an agony of bashfulness.

'*Bonsoir, Madame,*' he mumbles, gazing fixedly down at my slippers. 'Eliane has asked me to inform you that we're going to be butchering the pig tomorrow. If you would be prepared to come and assist us, then that would be greatly appreciated.'

I strain to understand what he's saying as his accent is pure *sud-ouest*, as chewy as a slice of *Tarte Tatin*. He uses the formal '*vous*', and it sounds as if he's been rehearsing this speech on his way over here, probably dragging his feet reluctantly, having been sent by Eliane on this terrifying errand.

I reach out my hand and shake his large paw. '*Bonsoir, Mathieu.* It would be a pleasure. What time shall I come?'

'About nine o'clock? We start earlier, but the preliminary preparations we will handle ourselves.'

I suspect these 'preliminary preparations' involve doing the dire and dreadful deed itself and—call me a coward—I'm secretly relieved that I won't have to witness it. I've really grown quite fond of that pig, becoming used to his appearances as he totters into sight across the lawn while I'm busy with my cooking.

And I'm pleased to think that at least he's had several feasts of my gently fermenting apples to cheer his twilight days.

'We'll be in the old scullery, round the back of the house.'

'Okay, I'll come find you about nine. *A demain.*'

He shambles off, settling the cap back onto his grizzled head, and disappears back across the yard at some speed, clearly relieved to have delivered Eliane's message.

◆ ◆ ◆

The scullery must once have been a dwelling in its own right, before the farmer's cottage was added on in front. It looks positively mediaeval: a dark, cavernous room with low-slung, smoke-blackened beams that skim the top of Mathieu's head. The floor is uneven beneath our feet, but its ancient clay tiles have been scrubbed until they're spotlessly clean. The rough walls are freshly whitewashed and there's a long trestle table in the centre of the room, whose pine top is bleached from years of thorough scouring. Against one wall there's a vast stone fireplace, tall enough for me to stand in, where a lively fire crackles beneath an iron pot that looks like a witch's cauldron.

Eliane, wearing a clean apron, comes to kiss me as I peer tentatively in through the open doorway, and Mathieu raises one bear-like paw in greeting, brandishing a serious-looking butcher's knife whose long steel blade glints, sharp as a razor, in the firelight.

One half of my old porcine friend is hanging from a beam near the door, where the chill air keeps it cool. Mathieu is busy carving the other half of the carcass into neat sections. He wields the knife with precision, delicately, almost as an artist would wield a paintbrush, and I watch, fascinated, forgetting to feel squeamish as I watch the single slab of meat become transformed into cuts that would look familiar on a butcher's counter.

Eliane explains what is involved in preparing each different part so that the meat can be stored to keep them going through the coming year. We need to cure the hams, packing them with salt, pepper and bay berries before wrapping them in muslin; they'll be hung in a cool, dark corner to dry for several months, until they're ready to be served in wafer-thin slices with summer salads. The main cuts for roasting, or for making into tasty stews and *carbonnades*, can simply be wrapped up and put in the freezer for future use. But most of the work is in mincing up all the scraps that are left over and using them to make pâtés and sausages. Every single part of the animal is used so that not a thing goes to waste. The scraps that are too fatty to put through the mincer are thrown into the cauldron and slowly rendered down so that, by the end of the day, we have several large jars of pure white lard which Eliane will use for cooking. And even the tiny scraps of leaner meat, that are skimmed out of the cauldron once this fat has melted, are packed into jars to be eaten with hunks of bread. 'We call these *grattons*,' Eliane explains. I've seen them in charcuteries before, but never knew exactly what they were.

We make yards of sausages, flavoured with onions, and thyme, sage and fennel seeds from the *potager* (the herbs are my suggestion), and add garlic and seasoning to the minced meat to make farmhouse pâté. Once the mixture has been packed into jars, each with its rubber seal, and the glass lids wired tightly shut, the pâtés are stacked into a large pressure cooker that Eliane has sitting ready on top of her stove in the kitchen. She fills it with water to cover the jars and then slots the top onto the pot, screwing down the lid so that the steam can't escape, other than through the valve that regulates the pressure, and ensuring that the pâtés will be cooked thoroughly at a high temperature.

We work all through the day, pausing only for a lunch of *jimboura*, a surprisingly delicious broth made from the water which has been used to cook the black puddings (yes, we even used the blood!) and then had carrots, leeks and cabbage added to make a filling soup. Mathieu uncorks a bottle of red wine and pours generous glasses for each of us.

'Oh, this is all so good,' I exclaim as I mop my soup plate with a crust of bread.

'You won't find dishes like this in any restaurant these days,' Eliane observes. 'Traditional cooking has all but died out. Everyone is in such a hurry nowadays, wanting to cut corners and use ready-made stock or instant sauces. Whatever happened to taking your time, making simple food with love and a true understanding of the ingredients? You know,' she continues, fixing me with her clear gaze, 'there's scope for someone to open a really good traditional bistro around here. Rose tells me you used to run such a restaurant in London.'

I nod. 'I learnt my cooking from my grandmother and she was a woman after your own heart. When I was at the cookery school in Paris, we studied traditional French cuisine. You're right; there's a good deal to be said for a return to the old ways, cooking seasonal, local food. Better for the planet as well.'

I should have known better than to mention global warming, even obliquely, because Eliane launches into another diatribe about the very bizarre weather that we're having nowadays, accompanied by frequent sighs and shakings of the head from Mathieu as he ladles more *jimboura* into his bowl from the china tureen on the table in front of us.

To try and distract them from the doom and gloom, I ask, 'Do you ever name your pigs?'

Eliane shakes her head firmly. 'No, it wouldn't do to name something that we were going to end up eating.'

Mathieu raises his head. 'Tell her about the President.' He gestures with his spoon and then tips a little rough red wine from his glass into his bowl to help flush out the last dregs of soup, which he relishes with another appreciative slurp.

Eliane grins. 'Ah, yes, that was a good story! The mayor of a neighbouring commune, over at Coulliac I think it was, decided to name his pig one year and called it *Le Président*. When the time came to butcher it, he was having a drink at a bar with some friends and was overheard saying, "So who will come and give me a hand tomorrow. We're going to be killing *Le Président*." Well, of course, someone overheard and the next thing the mayor knew, he had a posse of policemen on his doorstep demanding to know what he was up to and saying they were there to prevent a *coup d'état*! He had a hard time explaining his way out of that one, until he took the *gendarmes* to the sty and introduced them to his pig in person.'

Mathieu guffaws appreciatively, slapping his hand on the table.

'Ah, yes,' I say, nodding gravely, 'I can see that naming one's pig could be fraught with jeopardy.'

After we've consumed the best part of a wheel of creamy camembert, Mathieu uncorks an unlabelled bottle of deep gold liquid. '*Mademoiselle Evie, un petit Armagnac?*'

I allow him to pour a little into my glass and take a sip, trying not to gasp as the firewater burns my throat. It's certainly fortifying, and fleetingly I give thanks that Mathieu's work with those lethally sharp butcher's knives is pretty much finished for the day. As he makes to refill my glass, I shake my head with a laugh and put a hand over the top of it. '*Merci,* but I'd better not... or I might be arrested for a new criminal offense: drunk in charge of a mincing machine!'

Perhaps it's the Armagnac that loosens my tongue, or perhaps it's the memories of cooking alongside my grandmother that this day is conjuring up but, as Eliane and I work side by side that afternoon, I find myself telling her about the years in Paris and London. She asks about the bistro, enthusing about the dishes we used to serve. Pausing as she lifts jars of pâté out of the pressure cooker and sets them on a rack to cool, she glances at me appraisingly.

'You know, Evie, your eyes really shine when you talk about your work. You must miss it?'

And I nod slowly as I realise that, for the first time in a long while, I really do.

Seeing myself through Eliane's eyes—in my element as I chop and stir and adjust a seasoning here and there—suddenly I understand that losing Lucie was only a part of my bereavement. A major part, of course. But losing my work was another blow. I hadn't realised until now, working in Eliane and Mathieu's rudimentary kitchen, that my cooking is such a fundamental part of me. It's how I best express myself: it's my heart and soul. And today has given me back some of the sense of self that the events of the past year had taken from me.

I leave at the end of the day, breathing in the crisp evening air as the huge crimson sun sinks below the horizon. On one arm I'm carrying a basket, into which Eliane has packed several chops, a couple of pounds of sausages, some links of *boudin noir*, and three jars of pâté. And under the other arm I've got the pressure cooker, which I've borrowed from Eliane in order to cook a Christmas Pudding in double-quick time.

It's been a satisfying day's work...

Although I do think I might just make myself some vegetarian pasta for supper tonight, as a welcome contrast to all those mountains of meat.

◆ ◆ ◆

Didier is leaning against the kitchen counter, savouring a glass of well-chilled Bordeaux *blanc* as he watches me preparing our supper. I've spent the afternoon making the Not-Christmas Pudding, chopping and soaking dried fruit, stirring the ingredients together and letting the whole lot steep in a generous splash of amber cognac, which hasn't had to travel very far from its home just to the north of us. I couldn't find all the dried fruit that my recipe calls for, but I've experimented a little by using some plump Agen prunes in place of currants, which I hope will enrich the mix in lieu of a month or so of maturing. The pudding is now in the pressure cooker, which is just starting to get up a head of steam on the stove.

Tonight's supper, since you are so kind as to ask, is going to be simplicity itself: some of the home-made sausages from yesterday, served with fluffy mashed potatoes which have had a generous dollop of who-legrain mustard stirred through them to add a little piquancy. And, in a nod to my Irish roots as well, I've shredded some dark, leathery leaves of Savoy cabbage which I'll steam, so they still have a little crunch when I dish them up, as green as Galway grass, alongside the sausage and mash.

Couldn't be simpler. But then, as *Mamie* Lucie used to say, the best meals are those seasoned with friendship and conversation. And, I might add, if the seasoning happens to bear a striking resemblance to Bradley Cooper then *tant mieux*. I realise, too, that a major part of regaining my love of cooking lies in preparing food for others. There seems so much more point to it than to half-heartedly cobbling together something for myself alone.

We're just finishing the main course, and I'm in full flow describing yesterday's butchery master class, when suddenly there's a violent rattling noise from the pressure cooker. I notice that the steady plume of steam that has been streaming from the safety valve on the lid has disappeared. The valve must have jammed shut and now the pot has built up so much pressure that it's in danger of exploding if I don't act fast. I leap up, turn off the heat under the pot, wrap a dish towel around my hand and grab a long-handled wooden spoon so that I can give the valve a brisk tap without risking scalding myself. There's a loud, hissing sigh of relief as the valve releases and a cloud of the trapped steam escapes, condensing into water droplets on the cooker hood above. As the steam clears, I take the dish towel and mop the water away. Checking my watch, I figure the pudding's probably cooked long enough for now anyway and can sit happily in the pot until it's finally cooled.

Didier is watching closely. 'Wow, I didn't realise Christmas Puddings could be so dangerous! What was that you just did?'

I tell him how the pressure-release valve works, shaking out the damp dish cloth and draping it over the handle of the oven door to dry. As I explain, a strange look comes over his face. And then he suddenly leaps up from the table, grabs me, hugs me tightly and plants a smacking kiss on my forehead.

Excitable people, these French. Who'd have thought a simple lesson in the correct use of cooking paraphernalia could cause such an ecstatic response? Note to self: must try and think of a few more items of kitchen equipment to demonstrate to him—the blender, perhaps, and the electric whisk: who knows *where* it could lead...

'Of course!' he cries. 'Evie, *merci*, you are a genius.'

I demur politely, somewhat mystified as to exactly what I've done to warrant this accolade, but I guess I'll take any compliments that are going.

'Come!' He takes me by the hand and leads me out into the yard, where the horse peers out at us over her stable door, disturbed by the sudden commotion. 'Wait there!' Didier leaves me standing outside the garage, its frosted windows dark. He reappears at a run, with the key.

Pushing open the door, I step into the gloom and blink as he switches on the harsh overhead lights. It's a real man-cave, a workshop with tools strewn everywhere. Standing in the middle of the floor is a strange contraption, about the size and shape of a two-drawer file cabinet, but with a complicated tangle of wires and leads and tubes protruding from the back. On the top perches an electronic screen, and what looks like a small accordion is fixed to the side... Some kind of musical instrument maybe?

'O-kay?' I'm not sure what to say really. Let's start with, 'What is it?'

'This, my dear Evie, is an anaesthesia machine. But, unlike most other anaesthesia machines, this one is very simple to operate; it will keep on running when the power cuts out; and it doesn't require large, expensive bottles of pressurised gas. It's an anaesthesia machine that will save lives in the places where it's needed most, in war zones and refugee camps. And,' he hugs me again, 'thanks to you and your Christmas

Pudding, we have now solved one of the final problems with the design.'

'Well, you're welcome. I'm very glad to be of help. Cooking, complicated medical science, it's all in a day's work really.'

He lets go of me—(oh no! I was enjoying that hug)—and picks up a length of clear plastic tubing.

'You see, my very clever machine concentrates oxygen from the air around us, which has the advantage of being both plentiful and free; hence, no need to rely on expensive cylinders of compressed gas, which run out or don't even turn up in the first place. But now, say it's the rainy season in Africa. The air is full of humidity. We want the air, but we don't want the water vapour that it holds because it can affect the workings of the machine. My problem is: how do we remove the water vapour? And the answer, as you have so clearly demonstrated, lies in changing the pressure. I need to make the system simple, yet at the same time as resilient as possible, so instead of a sophisticated valve such as you have on your pressure cooker, I think I can make a condensing area here'—he gestures to a length of plastic tubing that projects from the side of the machine—'by adding on a section of this wider-gauge tubing.'

I look at him blankly. 'And that will solve the problem because...?'

'Because the oxygen-enriched air that travels down this tube is under pressure. So when it encounters the wider tube, the pressure drops suddenly and—*eh hop!*—the water will condense out, just as that cloud of steam condensed when you hit the release valve on the cooking pot.' He grabs a pencil and notepad and begins sketching out how it might work. 'I'll need the right connectors, a T-junction in the tubing to drain the water away into some kind of reservoir, *tac, tac, tac...*' He puts down the pad and beams at me. 'It should work. No, even better—it *will* work!'

I look about me. So *this* is what he gets up to late at night. He's hard at work, saving the world. As one does, hidden away in the depths of rural France. Hold the presses: the guy turns out to be even more amazing than we first thought!

The cement floor is beginning to feel positively arctic beneath the thin soles of my indoor shoes and I pull the edges of my sweater about me with a shiver, having come outside so precipitously without the time to grab a coat. Didier is sorting through a jar of widgets, or gizmos, or possibly whatchamacallits, and looks as though he might be settling in for an all-night session unless I can come up with some sort of distraction. I touch his arm gently.

'Perhaps this can wait until tomorrow? Because right now I propose we go back inside, where it's warm, so that we can finish our meal and I can ask you, as we eat the pear and almond tart that I've made for dessert, how come a rural locum doctor is busy inventing a complex and fascinating anaesthesia machine for use in the third world in his garage.'

'But of course! Evie, you are freezing.' He switches off the lights and locks the door behind us.

As we cross the courtyard, our breath condensing in the chilly night air, the thirteenth moon hangs heavy behind the oaks, approaching fullness. Perhaps it's something to do with the cold air, but its colour has changed from the usual bright gold to a burnished copper, casting an ominous, rust-tainted light over the frosty ground. A ball of mistletoe is silhouetted against the pockmarked orange orb. I half expect a witch on a broomstick to fly across it—there's a hint of sinister bewitchment in the air tonight. Eliane's superstitions must be getting to me, I chide myself silently...

Back in the comfort of the bright, warm kitchen, the pressure cooker is murmuring quietly to itself as the pudding cools on the stove. We settle ourselves back down at the table and I cut each of us a generous slice of pear tart, the buttery pastry crumbling as I slice into it. I push a bowl of *crème fraîche* towards Didier.

'Now, spill the beans. So, apart from a need to escape Christmas, what brought you here and inspired you to invent that machine?'

At first he seems reluctant to talk, sitting in silence and gazing, unseeing, at the dessert plate before him. But then, as if the warmth of the kitchen has finally begun to thaw the permafrost that's gripped his heart since he lost Aurélie, he picks up his fork and takes a bite. And maybe it's the comfort of good food, prepared with love, but the thaw allows his words to flow freely at long last, his story pouring forth like spring meltwater.

'Well, to begin at the beginning, I suppose you have to go back three years. To the Christmas of Aurélie's death. We'd planned to spend the day with our families, her parents and mine celebrating together, looking forward to our wedding in the spring. So you can imagine how terrible that was, being preoccupied with funeral arrangements instead, everything closed over Christmas so we had to prolong the agony of waiting, having to tell everyone, ruining so many Christmases with the sad news. And even after the funeral, I still had the date we'd planned for the wedding looming ahead of me like a brick wall, overshadowing every day of my life. I was working as an anaesthetist at a large teaching hospital in Paris—that's my specialism, you see. But I just wanted to run away, as far and as fast as I could, somewhere where I didn't have to see the sorrow on the faces of Aurélie's parents, my own parents, all our friends... On a staff notice board at the hospital there was some information about *Médecins Sans Frontières*. Have you heard of them?

I nod. 'Doctors Without Borders? Of course, it's a fantastic organisation. I know they do incredible work, sending medical staff to wherever there's a crisis in the world.'

'Well, I phoned up, applied straight away, took compassionate leave from work and, because I said I was prepared to go absolutely anywhere at very short notice, I found myself in a refugee camp in South Sudan. The world's newest country. It had only just been created, after years of war in the region. It's still turbulent there now: tribes at war with each other; the fighting raging on. More than half a million people have had to flee their homes. And conditions are harsh. Poverty, fear, disease. They have one of the highest infant mortality rates in the world. Not to mention *the* highest maternal mortality rate.' He points his fork at me. 'If you're a pregnant South Sudanese woman, you have a one in seven chance of dying in childbirth.'

'That's horrific,' I say, suddenly not hungry at all. I push my plate away.

His expression, which had hardened at the memories of the challenges he'd had to face in Africa, softens as he notices my sudden loss of appetite.

'Oh, I'm sorry, Evie, that was tactless of me.'

I shake my head. 'No, Didier, I wasn't thinking about my own pregnancy. I was thinking of Tess, my sister. But I know she's in good hands. Both her experience and my own must be so different from anything those women have to go through.'

And in any case, this conversation isn't about me. It's about him. I can see from the strain that shows in the lines of his face that it's hard for him to talk about these things. But I now understand how important it is for him to do so. Swallowing my anxiety for my little sister, I pick up my fork again and smile at him, encouragingly. 'Please, go on…'

'So there I was, working in a makeshift hospital in one of the biggest refugee camps, just outside Juba. It was certainly a change of scene. And it succeeded in my aim of distracting myself from Aurélie's death. Most days I worked non-stop and then collapsed onto a camp-cot in a dusty tent for a few hours' sleep before getting up to do it all over again. We were fighting to save the lives of the injured and maimed who managed to make it to the hospital, as well as waging our own war against epidemics of cholera, TB, black fever, with very few resources.'

'But what about international aid? Couldn't they help? Give you more resources, more equipment?'

He shakes his head, sorrowfully. 'Let me give you an example to help you understand the problems we faced out there. In the hospital, I had a state-of-the-art anaesthesia machine, not unlike the ones I was used to using in the hospital in Paris. But I could only use it when the electricity was on, which was never a given. We'd be in the middle of an operation and there'd be a power cut. And if I did have power then, often, the bottles of compressed gas would run out, even though I was constantly ordering more supplies; they either never got delivered or turned out to be empty bottles which had de-pressurised because the valves were faulty. I could never count on having enough gas available.'

'You must have seen some terrible things there,' I murmur quietly, sobered by his story.

He nods, his blue eyes clouded with the memories of things he'd witnessed. Little lines of pain etched across his forehead. For a moment I worry that he's going to clam up again, slamming the door shut on those memories that are still too painful to handle. But at last he focuses his gaze on my face again and finds the strength to go on.

'And then, disaster struck. An even worse disaster, that is, on top of the disaster zone it already was. It was another December—coming up to Christmas again. Somehow these things are all the more grotesque in that context. There had been tribal clashes in Jonglei, the neighbouring state to the one I was in, and there was a raid on an MSF clinic in a town called Pibor. They killed hundreds, including members of staff. One was a good friend of mine. In Africa's dark heart, it was one of the darkest moments of all. They pulled us out, all international MSF staff, fearful that there'd be more such raids. They've gone back in again now, but at the time we had to desert those poor people, leaving them to survive as best they could. I came home to France. I needed a rest after all those months of gruelling work, all the trauma. I was exhausted. I'd scarcely taken any leave in the two years I'd been there and I'd overdone it too, I suppose, trying to forget my own misery by saving others. Not having to think about losing Aurélie as long as I was distracting myself, day after day, with other people's problems, other people's misery. My parents were worried about me. And so that was when I decided to try another change of scene for a while, come down here just until I'm strong enough to go back to Africa again. Through a family friend, I heard that old Doctor Lebrun was retiring, but that the commune had been unable to find a replacement. It seemed a good opportunity to hide away from the world for a while and regroup.' He shrugs.

We sit in silence for a minute or two, each lost in our own thoughts.

And then I say, 'So your way of regrouping is to spend every night building a machine that will help those people you left behind in South Sudan—and everywhere else that there's a need for anaesthesia under such terrible conditions.'

I reach out and put my hand on his, so that he will know how profoundly his story has moved me.

'The priest in the church said to me that we should try to do what we can to let a light shine out in the darkness. Your story is amazing, Didier. You're trying to light up the whole world. Working so hard to save so many lives.'

He raises his eyes to mine. And then his strong fingers close around mine, holding on tight.

'No,' he says quietly. 'I think maybe I'm working so hard to save my own.'

◆ ◆ ◆

It's another glorious morning, bright and clear with a scattering of silver frost; across one corner of the window, the delicate lace of a spider's web is traced in sparkling white, as if someone's come along in the night and shaken out one of those tubes of glitter that Tess and I used to make homemade Christmas cards with when we were little. We'd sit at the kitchen table cutting out lacy snowflakes from folded squares of paper and then dot them with glue and sprinkle on the glitter, shaking off the excess onto a tray so that it could be scooped up and used again. Then we'd paste the intricate shapes onto bright-coloured card. We'd work side by side, in companionable silence, sharing the scissors and the glue pot, occasionally glancing over to admire each other's work. And in the background, *Mamie* Lucie would potter at the stove, filling the air around us with heady scents of cloves and cinnamon as she prepared her Christmas baking. I remember how Tess, two years younger than me, would try so hard to make her snowflakes as intricate and neat as mine, the tip of her tongue poking out of the corner of her lips as she concentrated on manoeuvring the scissors.

My heart lurches suddenly, with love for my little sister. I wish I could wrap my arms around her and give her a big hug. I miss her so much. And there's so much we should be sharing now. I should be there to support her, but I guess I'll have to make do with hiking up the hill later on and sending her a message...

I pick up the heavy pressure cooker that I borrowed from Eliane, which I'm going to return to her now that the pudding's three-quarters cooked. I'll finish it on the day by simmering it for another couple of hours in a normal pan.

I find her working in her garden at the back of the cottage. She's hoeing the dark soil, keeping the weeds out. There's a wicker trug of produce beside the neatly dug bed, containing some tender baby leeks, some salad leaves and other greenery that I don't recognise. At my appearance, she pauses, smiling, and pushes a few strands of her fine, white hair away from her face with the back of her hand.

I kiss her on both cheeks. 'Your pressure cooker. Thanks for the loan, Eliane.'

'Your Pudding *de Noël* is made then? Was it a success?'

'We'll only know on the day when it's had its final boiling and is ready to eat. I had to adjust the recipe a bit, though, so who knows? Are you and Mathieu doing anything Christmas Day? If not, I'd love it if you'd join me for lunch. Didier will be there too. But I guess you'll probably be spending it with your family?'

'You mean on the twenty-fifth? Actually, no. Here in France we have our big celebrations *en famille* on the night of the twenty-fourth of December. We call it *Réveillon*. Mathieu and I will be going to my sister, Mireille's, for dinner that evening. She has four sons, three of whom are married, and ten grandchildren, so it'll be quite a party! But on the twenty-fifth we normally just have a quiet day à *deux*. So, yes, thank you, Evie, we'd love to join you and have a chance to sample this famous pudding of yours.'

'So you and Mathieu don't have any children of your own? Or do they live elsewhere?'

Eliane gazes off into the distance and I get the impression that her clear grey eyes seem to be watching scenes that only she can see. The wind gusts suddenly, blowing strands of hair across her face, but this time she doesn't push them away. Her expression is so sad that it speaks volumes.

'Sorry,' I apologise, kicking myself. I, of all people, should know to be more sensitive when it comes to asking that question. Time was, in the early days after losing Lucie, I couldn't even begin to find the words to express my loss, so naturally my friends

and my family stopped mentioning her altogether…
Although I sometimes used to wish people *would* still
ask, instead of awkwardly skirting around the issue, so
that I could have talked about Lucie, painful though
it might have been. At least it would have been an
acknowledgement that she'd existed. And now I
understand that it might have given me a chance to
work through a little more of my pain too—the same
pain I see written in Eliane's expression.

She turns back to me. 'Come,' she says, propping
the hoe against a fence post. 'And leave that pot here.'

We walk up the driveway that leads past the cottage
to the château up on the hill, but halfway up, we turn
off it, onto a small path worn through the grasses that
bow and bend their heads as the wind, which seems
to be getting up a little now, brushes past them. The
path leads up along one side of the vineyard, towards
the wooded crest of the hill. Just below the trees,
there's a whitewashed wall enclosing a small square of
land. I assume it must be an old sheep-pen or something. But Eliane pushes open a little wooden gate set
into the wall and suddenly we're standing in a tiny
graveyard.

Half a dozen simple gravestones are clustered
behind the shelter of the walls, in the embrace of the
dark trees on the hill behind. 'Pierre-Henri Castel.

Henri Jacques Castel. Mathilde Castel, née Leblanc,'
I read.

'These are the grandfather and parents of the
owner of the château,' Eliane explains. She leads
me to a side wall where several small plaques have
been set into the plaster. 'These are memorials to
Mathieu's father and brother. They died in the war.
And these,' pointing to three small white ovals, 'are
my children.'

'Mathieu Dubosq; Amélie Dubosq; Liliane
Dubosq.' I say each name carefully. There are no dates.

'I never managed to carry a child to full term. But
nonetheless I gave birth to each of them so they are
our children and we remember them here. So you
see, Evie, I understand a little of what you've gone
through.' She turns that clear gaze on me again,
seeing into my very soul. Then says, quietly, 'Rose
told me you lost your baby.'

My throat catches as I notice three fresh posies of
sweet-scented white hyacinths that have been laid
under each of the plaques.

'I come here often, to visit them and talk to them,
and bring them flowers. In summer, I bring honey-
suckle and roses; at this time of year, these hyacinths,
to remind us all that spring will come again. We just
have to wait it out. Just as the winter eventually passes,

so does our grief. You have to give it time, Evie. Time, and love. That's the only recipe for healing.'

I nod, unable to speak, as my throat is full of sudden emotion. I think of the basket of baking she left on my doorstep to mark St Nicolas's Day, which has new significance now. Perhaps it's her way of comforting herself, of entrusting her babies to the saint's care. What was it the priest said? *A simple, practical gesture of remembrance can be a balm for the soul when we are grieving.* I fumble in my pocket for a Kleenex and wipe away the tears that spill from my eyes.

'You will always carry your baby in your heart, Evie,' says Eliane, laying a hand on my arm. 'But, you know, the time will eventually come when you'll be able to set down the grief you've been carrying there too, and start living again. I believe we become the ambassadors in this world for our unborn children; it's our duty to live our lives to the full on their behalf, because we are living life for them as well. Otherwise death will have won. And we cannot let that happen.'

We stand together in silence for a while, each lost in our own thoughts.

Eventually, when I can speak again, I say, 'Why is it so hard to move on? I feel so stuck, Eliane. I'm not sure it's even so much to do with losing Lucie anymore. Lighting a candle in the church, and accepting that she's safe now, helped me begin to let go of my sadness. But I still feel so angry. Angry at Will, for not being there when I needed him the most. Angry at myself, too, I guess, for not being able to save Lucie.'

'Ah, anger,' she smiles sadly. 'Anger will weigh you down and eat away at you, eroding any chance you have of beginning to live again.'

I nod. 'That's exactly how it feels. Like I'm sinking into quicksand under this burden I'm carrying.'

'Sometimes we direct the anger we feel about things we can't control towards those who are closest to us. At the very people we love the most. That's where the power of anger is at its most destructive. For your own sake, you have to try to forgive. Forgive your husband. And, most importantly of all, forgive yourself. And yes, that is one of the hardest things of all. True forgiveness takes enormous strength and very great courage. A person who can forgive is one of the bravest people there is. It may seem impossible, but you have to do it, Evie. Even if it means you have to keep on trying to forgive, and go on forgiving again, every single day of your life.'

I shiver, despite the warm sun and the protection from the wind that the walls of the little graveyard offer.

Eliane smiles and takes my hand, squeezing it reassuringly, as if to help give me the strength that she knows I'm going to need. 'You are getting chilled. Let's go back down and have a cup of *tisane*.'

We walk back towards the cottage, the wind gusting, buffeting us, suddenly with a much colder edge to it. 'Look here,' Eliane beckons me into a little orchard of bare-twigged fruit trees set out in neat rows just above the vegetable patch. Three white wooden boxes with sloping roofs, like dolls' houses, sit here raised on bricks. 'My bees. Listen.' She presses her ear to the side of one, and I do the same. There's a low hum, deep in the belly of the hive, like a faint engine. 'They sit out the cold, retreating into the heart of the hive, where they cluster together around the queen for warmth. The worker bees flutter their wings and move their bodies constantly to generate enough heat to help the swarm survive. They know that if they can just keep going through the cold, one day summer will come. They couldn't survive as individuals, but together, as a community, they get each other through the tough times. A good example to us humans.' She smiles her gentle smile, making me feel a part of *this* community, grateful to her and Mathieu and Didier, these new friends who have helped me, in their different ways, to keep warm in the depths of winter;

to keep alive the hope that, some day, summer will return.

As we pass by the vegetable patch, Eliane scoops up the trug and the pot, carrying them into the kitchen.

'What are these?' I ask, pointing to some yellow-green leaves that nestle in her basket alongside a bunch of darker green lamb's lettuce, grateful for the distraction in the wake of so much emotion in that little graveyard up the hill. 'I don't recognise them.'

'Around here, we call this *navet des vignes*. I don't know its scientific name, nor what you'd call it in English.'

'*Navet*? That means turnip. So "turnip of the vines". How curious!'

'It's delicious, and in fact it does taste a little like turnips. I'll cook it in a savoury tart with eggs and cheese and serve it with a salad of this *mâche*.' She gestures to the leaves of lamb's lettuce. 'All of this I picked in the vineyard this morning. They grow wild there. Food for free.'

'What, these baby leeks too?'

She nods. 'We call these *aillet*. You use them as you would normal leeks. But,' she frowns, her expression severe, 'you know, they really shouldn't be here at this time of the year. It shows how crazy the weather's been this year. Normally I'd be picking all of these in the spring, in April or even May. These poor plants have got confused with the cold, wet autumn we had and then these warm days now. They very foolishly poked their heads above the ground far too early. I've been gathering them this morning before the storm arrives, when, I fear, all will be lost.'

There she goes again with the doom and the gloom! Sipping my steaming cup of *verveine* tea, I glance out at the window to where Bruno the dog lies asleep in a sheltered, sunny corner of the yard, his tongue lolling and his long tail flicking the dusty ground with an occasional twitch as he dreams of chasing rabbits.

'What makes you think there's going to be a storm? I checked the forecast a few days ago and the weather seems to be set fair.'

She shakes her head. 'Pah! What do they know? These forecasters who sit in their windowless offices in front of their computer screens! You know how I've explained to you about the thirteenth moon? Well, even worse, now it's a *lune rousse*, a red moon.'

I remember the moon from that evening with Didier, and nod. 'I noticed. It *did* look kind of rust-coloured the other night.'

'*Précisément*. Which foretells bad weather to come. You mark my words, Evie, there's a storm on the way. The birds know. When you go for your next walk up the hill, see if you can spot any of the usual birds of prey up there. This morning, when I was gathering this produce in the vines, there wasn't a single one to be seen, not a buzzard nor a red kite. Even the crows have flown off. And if anyone knows, apart from the moon itself of course, it's the birds. I've told Mathieu to bring the horse in and keep her in the barn now. It'll be her time to foal before too long and we don't want to risk it being born outside in stormy weather.'

As I take my leave from Eliane, she hugs me tight. 'Come and see me again soon, Evie. We can do some cooking together perhaps? Food always tastes more appetising when it's shared—the preparation and the eating.'

'I'd love that. I'll bring my grandmother's recipes to show you too. I'd like to try out some more of them and you'll be able to show me how they should really be made.'

I set off up the hill to check my emails, raising my face to the clear blue sky above. The wind snatches at my hair and my jacket, teasing and goading, like a bored child who can't resist making mischief. I settle down, my back to the solid face of the milestone, and re-check the weather forecast. The temperatures seem to be down a bit and the wind a little more lively, but nothing more than that. It's still predicting sunny days. I glance into the blue of the sky that arches over me. Eliane was right about the birds though. Nothing moves there, apart from the bare branches of the trees, to which the wind has now turned its attention, shoving and shaking, and making the fronds of mistletoe shimmy as they shiver in its teasing gusts.

The mistletoe reminds me of that New Year's Eve party in Paris, all those lifetimes ago, at the apartment of one of our fellow students from the cookery school. She was a Swiss girl, whose parents had a *pied-à-terre* in the elegant Sixteenth *Arrondissement,* far more sumptuous than my own tiny attic shoebox. We stood in the elegant, high-ceilinged reception room, beneath sparkling chandeliers, dressed in our glad rags, self-consciously trying not to catch sight of our reflections which appeared at unexpected moments in the vast mirrors at either end of the room.

Very soon though, after a few glasses of party cheer, all self-consciousness was forgotten. The laughter level rose along with the temperature as more and more guests arrived, and soon we were crammed in, part of a jostling throng. Will had to shout to make himself heard as someone turned up the music, and I leaned in close to make out what he was saying. He was always popular, the good-looking joker of our group of friends, and that night, as ever, he was glowing with the attention, in his element as party-animal-in-chief.

And I, young, naïve, far from home for the first time in my life, was seduced by the fact that he had chosen *me*. We shared a zest for life and a passion for cooking and we were so in love, there in the world's most romantic city. It was all perfect.

At midnight, as the countdown started, he pulled me to him under a bunch of mistletoe that hung in one of the tall window bays, and he kissed me as the clocks chimed and the room erupted in cheers. He leant in and whispered something in my ear. I couldn't quite hear what he said over the excited hubbub all around us, as so many beautiful young people heralded in the New Year and a future where everything was possible.

I put a hand behind my ear, turning my head to hear him more clearly as he whispered again.

'Marry me!'

I stepped back in amazement and gazed at his handsome face, his eyes glittering with the same delight that flooded my body. I took it all in for a moment, suspended in time: I can see it all so clearly still. The elegant room, the mistletoe hanging above us, the Paris skyline framed in the window, fireworks sending up bursts of multicoloured stars into the night above the Bois de Boulogne. And, of course, I whispered back, 'Yes!'

On my bleak hilltop, I shiver as the balls of mistletoe in the bare trees wag their fingers in warning. I should have known. Because, yes, it was all so perfect. But that was the problem. It was so perfect that our relationship had never been tested. We were young, living in a golden bubble of joy and hope and possibility. We had no idea that, like the bubbles in the glasses of champagne that were thrust into our hands as we celebrated that night, ours would disappear too, popping when it met the real world outside, unable to withstand the pressures of life.

I think about what Eliane said in the graveyard above her cottage. About forgiveness. She's right, I realise. I probably have turned the helpless anger that I feel towards myself—or, more accurately, towards the universe over which I have no control—against Will. And, impossible though it may seem, I need to try and let it go. For my own sake, as much as for anyone else's.

I hesitate, then type Will's name into Google. The screen on my phone fills with listings, reviews, photos, interviews with the new rising star of celebrity chefs. He seems in his element again, just as he was in our student days. Prince William. The centre of attention.

And I know it's not too late. I could be part of it too. He said so all along, urging me to get up out of bed when I lay there, poleaxed by grief, to come join him in the kitchen; to take an interest in the offer we'd received for the bistro; to help him decide whether to risk pursuing the route to a possible career in television or whether to carry on building the success of our restaurant...

But I couldn't. I couldn't focus. I couldn't decide. I couldn't summon up the energy to lift my head from the pillow, let alone get up and get going again. I was marooned in the fog of my depression, postnatal hormones running riot. And so, reluctantly, he reached out and grabbed the life preserver that was being held out to him, saving himself. Because he couldn't save me. He couldn't save *us*.

That last day, the day when he came to tell me that he'd made his decision, to go live up north for a while, closer to the TV studios, because he'd be so busy with the filming, I recall with shame. For a few, searing moments, I was filled with a blinding rage as I wrapped all of my pain up into a ball and hurled it at him. '*Go then*!' I screamed. 'You're never here anyway. You weren't here when I needed you. So *go*!'

He didn't even reply, just hung his head, bowing under the weight of his guilt and the storm surge of my anger. Stranded there in his own pain and sadness too. Each of us immersed in our shared grief, but unable to offer comfort to the other. I said some terrible things that day; I can understand why he left.

Yes, I can understand. But forgive? Well, I guess I need to keep working on it. And, as Eliane said, maybe I'll have to go on working on it every single day of my life. And hope, too, that one day he'll be able to forgive me back.

I scroll down the list of articles that mention Will, choose an interview from one of the Sunday newspapers and read it through. One particular paragraph catches my attention. "I owe so much to my wife, Evie. She and I started the restaurant together and she is an incredibly talented chef in her own right. It's a great sadness to me that we're not still together..." I re-read the words, letting them sink in. It seems like he's holding out an olive branch. When he said those words, did he hope I might read them, somewhere, somehow?

Darn this combination of the cold wind and my muddled emotions! I fumble for a Kleenex and blow my nose.

So. Forgiveness, hey? I guess I have to start somewhere.

Taking a deep breath, I type a brief email.

To: Will Brooke
Subject: Congratulations
Dear Will, just wanted to congratulate you on the programme's success. Am so pleased for you.
Love, Evie.

Before I can think too much and delete it, I hit 'send'. Then, quickly, switch off my phone and shove it deep into my pocket.

My legs are cold and stiff and I lean on the milestone to haul myself up, stomping my feet on the cold ground to get some circulation back into my frozen toes. I gaze at the view for a moment, at the dead-looking, wizened vines and the bare branches of the trees, stark against the December sky.

And then, unbidden, Didier's face springs to mind. I remember his smile like the sunrise in a winter's sky and I remember his fingers closing around mine. Holding on to the hope that one day this winter will end, that spring will come eventually, that from the dead-looking branches soft green leaves will unfurl, the bare stems will blossom, life will return... No matter how impossible all of that might seem in the here and the now.

Chapter 7
In the Bleak Midwinter

In the bleak midwinter
Frosty wind made moan...

I pile a couple more logs on the fire, the flames leaping high and making a hushed roar in the chimney which competes with the gusting and buffeting of the wind outside. I'll need a cosy blaze tonight to keep the cold at bay, because the temperature has plummeted.

I go to the kitchen to make myself a cup of hot chocolate which will warm me to the core before I have to brave the chillier reaches of the house upstairs on my way to bed.

In the hallway, borne on the wind across the yard from the garage, a faint sound of drilling can be heard. Good grief, it must be freezing out there! I decide to make two cups of the warming hot chocolate and go see how the latest modifications to the anaesthesia machine are coming along.

Didier is so engrossed in his work that he doesn't notice me come in, balancing two fragrantly steaming mugs on a tray. I watch him for a moment, my heart melting like the tender centre of a hot chocolate soufflé at the sight of his handsome profile bent over the workbench as he concentrates on fitting two lengths of tubing together.

'Aha, Doctor Didier, that looks a little like a depressurising chamber for the removal of humidity, if I'm not mistaken,' I say, mock-seriously, and he glances up with a look of pure, unadulterated joy. At the sight of me? Or maybe just at the thought of a welcome break and some warming sustenance?

'You are correct in your surmise, Doctor Evie. We are going to call it the Evie Brooke Chamber, in honour of the talented woman who inspired the idea.'

'Cool. I've never had a de-pressuring chamber on an anaesthesia machine named after me before, but I guess there's always a first time.' I have to confess, I feel inordinately proud of my own small contribution to his project; it gives me a sense of having a stake in it, even if it is only a tiny one. 'Here, I thought you might need to be thawed out, working in these sub-zero temperatures.' I hand him one of the mugs.

He nods, slurping his drink appreciatively. 'You're so very kind. It *is* a little on the chilly side out here this evening. *Mon Dieu*, that's good hot chocolate. What's in it?'

'The secret is to put a couple of cinnamon sticks in with the milk as you heat it. It adds that certain *je ne sais quoi.*'

'Another of your grandmother's tips?'

I shake my head. 'Uh-uh, this one I came up with myself. How are you getting on here?'

'Great. In fact, I think we might be ready to try this out. How timely your visit is—I need a guinea pig.'

'Are you going to put me to sleep?' I have to confess, the idea freaks me out.

He shakes his head. 'Certainly not. We're just going to hook you up and let you breathe some nice oxygen-enriched air for a few minutes.'

'What will that do? Get me high?'

'No, I'm afraid not!' he laughs. 'You won't notice any difference at all. But we'll hitch you up like so'—he clips a plastic peg to the end of my index finger—'and monitor your blood's oxygen saturation level.'

He flicks a couple of switches and the machine whirrs into action.

'It sounds like someone breathing,' I exclaim.

'Exactly so,' he says. 'You see, the machine inhales air from the atmosphere around us here, and then it exhales it, having increased the oxygen in it, through here for you to breathe in.' He hands me a plastic mask which is attached to one of the lengths of tubing protruding from the guts of the machine. 'And now here'—he gestures to the electronic screen and I edge round so I can get a better view—'we see your heartbeat on this trace. And this figure here is your blood's oxygen saturation. You're currently running at ninety-nine percent—probably because it's so cold that your circulation's a little sluggish at your fingertips. Give it a few nice, deep breaths and it should go back up to one hundred.'

My heartbeat pulses across the screen as a zigzagging green line. I concentrate hard on breathing slowly, because standing so close to him is making my heart race a little, and it would be extremely embarrassing to have him see that playing out so obviously, on the screen in front of us.

He explains a few more aspects of the way it works and then, satisfied with the test, removes the mask from my mouth and the peg from my finger.

And, despite my best efforts to keep my breathing calm and slow, that giveaway green line suddenly begins to make steeper peaks and troughs when he touches my hair to remove the oxygen mask, tucking an unruly curl back in place behind my ear. And then he holds my hand in his to unclip the peg from my finger and the trace cavorts wildly, the pounding of my heart writ large for all to see. Gallantly, he pretends not to have noticed, although when our eyes meet, his seem to sparkle all the more brightly beneath the unforgiving glare of the bare light bulb hanging above our heads.

The heart-rate monitor flatlines suddenly and then fades to black as he shuts the machine down.

'Brilliant!' he declares, turning away to check the glass flask that's attached to the tubing on one side. 'A very well-behaved patient. And now let's see, yes, we have a tiny amount of water in the Evie Brooke reservoir. Of course, because the air's so cold tonight, it doesn't contain much water vapour, so this wouldn't be a problem under these conditions. But you can imagine in the African rainy season, in the heat and at about eighty percent humidity, we'd be collecting far more water, preventing it from ending up in the machine where it would clog up the works and make it rust.'

'Bravo!' I raise my cup in a toast. 'Here's to saving many, many lives with the Doctor Didier Dumas patent portable anaesthesia machine!'

He sighs. 'Well, maybe one day...' He sounds tired suddenly, defeated.

'What is it, Didier? Another technical glitch? Perhaps we can go experiment with more kitchen equipment to work out a solution?'

'Sorry, Evie, it's just that I've had another funding application turned down today. I don't know who else to turn to. Now we have something that actually works, I'd need funding support from a larger company to take it to the next stage. The established manufacturers don't want to know—obviously, because it has the potential to make their own technologies redundant, even though it could mean saving lives for far less money. And I can't find anyone else who's altruistic enough to risk their money on some crazy doctor's tin-pot invention that he's cobbled together in his garage. It's incredibly frustrating. Looks like I'm going to have to shelve the project, even though we're so much closer. Whatever happens, though, Africa is calling me back. At least there I'll be doing something, even if this dream'—he pats the silent machine—'has failed.'

'Well, at least you will have tried.' I'm trying to reassure him, but my words sound as hollow as his own disappointment, because a wave of sadness washes over me at the thought of him leaving. Suddenly I can't bear to think of him not being here, even though I know neither of us will be staying in the long run.

'True. I have tried. And we have to keep on trying. Doing what we can. Even if we fail and have to shelve our dreams from time to time. We move on.'

I nod, remembering Eliane's words the other day as we stood in the little graveyard up the hill. 'A wise woman once said that we are ambassadors in this world for the dead and that we should live our lives on their behalf, in order to conquer death.'

He smiles sadly. 'It's true. A good philosophy. I sometimes think every life I can save is one more to offset against Aurélie's death. But I don't know how many it will take until the score is settled. I'd hoped that, with this invention, I might stand a chance, at last, of feeling I was getting there; making such a difference that, finally, I'd find some salvation of sorts.'

'You know, Evie,' he continues, the words pouring out now, as if Eliane's words have unlocked something inside him, 'it's not really the thought of being able to save *lots* of lives; even if we could save just one with this machine then all the hours of work would have been worth it. When I was working in the camp near Juba, every refugee who arrived had their own personal story of trauma and terror and loss. Men, women, children... The first Christmas I was there, I witnessed a very different kind of Nativity story. It lodged in my mind, in particular, because the couple were called Joseph and Mary. Joseph and Mary Abuja. They had other tribal names of course, but Joseph and Mary were the English names they'd chosen for themselves. They walked into camp on Christmas Eve. They'd fled an attack on their village three days before and had walked, afraid for their lives, to try and reach the safety of the refugee camp, with only the clothes they had on their backs. No food, no water. And Mary was pregnant. But there were complications, and there was no doubt that her condition wasn't helped by the trauma she'd suffered. She went into labour, needed an emergency Caesarean to deliver her child safely. But we didn't have the resources. No anaesthesia, no room in the hospital when there were so many others who so badly needed our help. So, instead of a happy Christmas ending, I'm afraid her story ends in a makeshift grave on top of a dusty hilltop, where Joseph laid both his wife and her unborn child. I saw him up there, day in, day out, just sitting, as the sun beat down remorselessly on his head. Waiting for death to take him too. All hope gone.'

He pauses, remembering, little lines of sadness gathering at the corners of his clear blue eyes.

'So giving up on my machine means giving up on people like them. Women like Mary.'

I swallow down the tears that are threatening to spill from my own eyes. His story has brought back painful memories of losing my own baby and my heart bleeds for Mary, for her terror and her fear and her pain. All those things I experienced myself, although I was in a clean hospital with nurses and doctors at my bedside and modern pain relief to help me through. Hers must have been unbearable, before death took both her and her baby. Her story gives me new strength, a new sense of determination. 'Well, then, we mustn't give up. We need to keep hammering on doors, telling their story, until someone listens.'

He nods. 'You're right, Evie. I know you're right. Sorry, I'm just a bit tired and dispirited this evening.' He gestures at the machine. 'My enthusiasm has flatlined, temporarily, just like that trace did. But I'm sure I'll feel differently tomorrow. Ready to go into battle again.'

I collect up our cups as he tidies away a few tools on the workbench and switches off the lights.

We step out into the chill blast of the wind, which snatches at my breath, making my teeth chatter as we stand for a moment under the oaks, reluctant to say goodnight. The thirteenth moon of the year is completely full at last, a perfect circle, and almost the same colour as the russet apples strewn across the grass out back by the wind. A wisp of mistletoe in the lower branches just above us flutters over our heads. My hands are occupied by the cups and the tray, and the wind catches my hair and swirls it into my eyes. Didier smiles and leans in, gently brushing the curls away from my face.

And I'm not sure whether it's the cold that takes my breath away or that single moment, when time seems suspended, and the moon and the mistletoe both conspire in their invitation to kiss.

We stand there, and it seems as though the world joins me in holding its breath. Waiting.

But then Didier drops his hand to his side. 'Goodnight, Evie.' His voice is soft and low.

'Goodnight, Didier.'

And then I turn and head for my front door, pausing for a moment to glance back to where he stands, his eyes dark pools in the shadows, watching.

I lie in my lonely bed, listening to the wind buffeting the stone walls of the house, thinking of Didier lying in his own bed just a few dozen yards away, and wondering why we didn't kiss. Because, without discussing it, I know that we both sense a connection, a spark. The look in his eyes spoke volumes when he took my hand in his to remove the clip from my finger. And he must have seen the look in mine as my heartbeats wrote my feelings in green fluorescent light across the screen. And, I promise you hand on heart, for my part those feelings are something more than simple lust, now that I've discovered the hidden depths behind that movie star exterior.

But there's also a sense that we need to wait. A sense that we each have our own unfinished business to deal with. A sense that this could be something big: but we need to be certain that it's more than just two lost souls seeking refuge from life's storms.

The wind gusts and blusters, making the window frames rattle, and I pull the covers up around my ears to shut out the sound and try to sleep.

I'm still mulling this over the next morning when I stride out purposefully, making for my office at the top of the hill. I want to check and see if there's anything from Tess; and there's also a long-overdue email I need to send my mother.

Today the fretful wind has dropped away completely—so Eliane's dire predictions seem to have

missed the mark again—although the still air is so cold
it burns my lungs, and the little stream that runs in the
ditch alongside the road is frozen into a ribbon of ice, as
smooth and black as the surface of a New England lake
in winter. It reminds me of the first skating expedition
each year. First, Dad would take the auger out of the tool-
shed and step out, tentatively, onto the frozen surface.
Tess and I would watch from the shore, hopping from
foot to foot with a mixture of excitement and nerves
(*What if it's not thick enough? What if it cracks and he
disappears under the ice?*). Once it was pronounced safe,
he'd look up and nod. 'Okay, girls, skates on!'

With freezing fingers, having impatiently peeled off
our mittens, we'd do up our boots, pulling the laces
tight so that the skates became a seamless continuation
of our legs, as if we'd replaced our broad, earthbound
feet with those flashing, knife-edged blades. We'd totter
out onto the ice, clinging to each other for balance at
first and shrieking as we lurched and skidded for the
first few steps. Until, all of a sudden, the balance would
return, the newfound sense of freedom sending our
spirits soaring into the blue sky above us as we struck
out, spreading our wings, gliding effortlessly over the
dark depths that, only a few months ago, had been our
summer playground as we splashed and swam.

'Don't go too far out!' our mother would call, still struggling to pull on her own skates.

'It's okay, Kate, don't worry.' Dad would hug her and then kneel to help tie her boots. 'There's a good four inches of ice. It's as solid as cement.'

And we'd spread our arms wide and fly across the lake, trying arabesques and pirouettes and jumps, high on the pure, cold air, and adrenaline, and unaccustomed levels of winter sunlight as it reflected off the ice around us, our laughter echoing back to us from the lake's hemlock-clad hillsides.

Afterwards, we'd clamber back up to the house, our skates slung around our shoulders by their laces, and Tess, her cheeks rosy with cold air and exhilaration, would chatter nineteen to the dozen as we pushed open the porch door, peeling off our layers of outdoor clothing before stepping into the warm kitchen for hot chocolate and cookies...

It's silent at the top of the hill, and my memories of the sounds of our breathless laughter and Tess's voice evaporate into the stillness. The air is tinged with the faint scent of wood smoke from the chimneys of the houses below, as homely as cinnamon toast. Missing my sister—and my family and home—makes me feel even more alone up here. There's still not a bird to be heard nor seen. Perhaps they'll be back soon though, now that the wind's dropped.

As if conjured up by my thoughts of her, there's an email from Tess. She sounds so happy, and I smile as I read it, scrolling down to see the photo she's attached of herself wrapped in layers of winter woollens, which only serve to exaggerate the ample roundness of her bump, her baby warm and snug somewhere underneath all that. And, right at the end of the message, as if it's an afterthought—which belies the significance that she and I both know it carries—there's a PS. It says, '*We're not telling anyone else, but, because you're not just anyone else, I thought I'd tell you: it's a boy.*'

I place a hand over my heart as it swells with a mixture of emotions: a flicker of my own loss; a surge of relief, too, that, this time at least, Tess's baby isn't a straight replacement for Lucie; and then a wave of overwhelming joy that brings tears to my eyes. I'm going to have a nephew. And I'm going to love him with all my heart, because he's a part of my sister and she's an inseparable part of my life, just as I'm a part of hers. I understand, now, how Eliane has been able to forgive the universe, by finding joy in her wider family.

When I'm able to collect my thoughts, I re-read Tess's message. '*Stop hiding yourself away in deepest, darkest France,*' she's written. '*We miss you! Mom is in overdrive, decorating the house and writing lists of instructions for everyone. Dad and I are in dire need of reinforcements. Come home, it's not too late. Jump on a plane and get your butt back here!*

And, just for a moment, I feel a pang of homesickness that's so strong that I almost *do* run down the hill, jump into the car and head for the nearest airport. But then I look back at the little cluster of buildings below, where plumes of smoke rise from the chimneys of the three houses, and I can see Mathieu, with Bruno hot on his heels, crossing the road to feed the horse where she's safely stabled in the barn.

I shake my head and smile as I type a message back to Tess. '*Sorry, unfinished business here this year. But I promise we'll be together next Christmas. And I'm going to book a flight to be there for February so that I can greet my nephew on his arrival into the world.*'

You bet I am: it's what Lucie would have wanted me to do.

And then I pull down the hem of my coat, so that I can sit on it on the frozen ground, and settle myself more comfortably against the milestone, to compose a long and detailed email to my mother about—of all things!—the need for portable, reliable anaesthesia in the refugee camps of the world.

Chapter 8

See, Amid the Winter's Snow

See, amid the winter's snow,
Born for us on earth below...

There's something not quite right. Instead of the normal brightness streaming in through the roof light in the bedroom to wake me fully, usually some time after I've already been disturbed by the distant crowing of the rooster, I drift up from the depths of sleep and open my eyes to a soft, muted greyness. I lie for a moment, trying to get my bearings, reluctant to leave behind my dreams. I can't remember them clearly, but they've left me with a sense of something happy, dreams full of promise and potential rather than the dreams of loss and sadness that I've come to expect during the past year's hibernation.

As I lie there, listening and gazing up at the window above me, which seems to have become opaque overnight, the only sound is a bird's faint *a cappella* song, as pure as a choirboy's unbroken voice.

Realisation dawns.

I scramble out of bed and hop across the chilly floorboards, pulling on a pair of thick socks, running down the stairs to the hallway. Each window sill is covered with a perfect, plump cushion of snow and the yard is blanketed with white perfection, as yet undisturbed by any footprints. I throw open the door to the sitting room and gasp at the beauty of the view that awaits me there, framed by the French doors. The countryside has been magically transformed overnight into a true winter wonderland. And whilst the baubles may have been rudely shaken from my Not-Christmas tree by the wind, the snow has now graciously transformed it into something even more wonderful. Each branch, and every individual twig, has been covered with white velvet, and generously sprinkled with silver sequins, which sparkle wherever the morning sun illuminates them. And on the very top, puffing up his rosy chest and singing his heart out with the sheer joy of being alive in the midst of all this wonder, is the robin. My own tiny choirboy, serenading me with a song as beautiful as any Christmas carol.

I put my hands on my hips and shake my head. 'Okay, okay, I get it now,' I tell him.

Because it seems that, despite my very best efforts to the contrary, Christmas Happens.

No matter how far you run, no matter how hard you try to shut it out, it creeps up on you from behind and ambushes you with its beauty and its traditions and its pure, bloody-minded determination to remind the world about what's really important. Making a light shine at the darkest time of the year. Bringing joy, and hope, and abundance to counter sadness, and despair, and scarcity.

I fled to this quiet corner of a foreign country thinking I would find solace in a place where no one spoke my language, where I'd be alone with my grief. But, instead, this tiny community has drawn me out of myself, helping me to see things more clearly, to gain a new perspective on the things that really matter to me. Eliane and Mathieu have helped rekindle my love of cooking, my passion for sharing recipes with others and learning new ones in return. And with Didier I have talked and listened as we shared our evening meals together, each of us contributing in our own ways, each of us helping the other to begin to take the first faltering steps out of the winter of our grief and into the promise of spring beyond.

And Mother Nature, despite being so shabbily treated by the world at large so that now she has her own problems to contend with, has persisted in her efforts to make me see the beauty that's been there all along, but to which my grief had blinded me.

It's the day before Christmas Eve. It's not too late. I'm going to decorate the house up to the rafters, just as my mother and my sister will be doing back in Boston. Even though I'm not with them this year, I'll make them proud: I will shop for presents for my newfound friends, for Didier and Eliane and Mathieu; I'll get a juicy bone for Bruno and a bag of apples for the horse; I will buy enough food for a feast on Christmas Day as a way of giving thanks for all that these people have given me, for the way they've befriended me, for their kindness. And I'm going to turn on all the lights and build up the fire and light candles in every window so that, when night falls, the light floods out into the darkness.

There's so much to do. I run back upstairs to get dressed and put my plan into action.

◆ ◆ ◆

The first hitch, I discover, is that the power has gone out. The clock on the electric stove is frozen at four-ten and when I flick the switch on the kettle there's nothing. I build up the fire in the sitting room and huddle close to it as I eat a bowl of cereal. The refrigerator's off too, of course, but I set the plastic milk carton outside on the doorstep where it's cold enough to keep it fresh. I find a cooler with a lockable lid and put the butter and a couple of yoghurts and a jar of Eliane's pâté in there too, safe from any marauding animals. I leave the freezer shut, trying to keep the cold in so that the sausages that are stored in there won't de-frost. I don't have any way of cooking them either now, I realise. But hopefully the power cut will be short-lived.

I take out the Christmas menu that I drew up all those weeks ago when the first glimmer of culinary inspiration was reawakened within me by my original trip to the market. With Didier, Eliane and Mathieu invited to Christmas lunch, I'll need to get to the stores. I'd been putting it off, in no particular hurry to get the shopping done given the beautiful, calm days we'd been enjoying, and thinking it would be best to wait until now—the day before *R*éveillon—to get the very freshest produce possible.

I curl up in front of the fire and review my proposed menu, making a few changes here and there, with *Mamie* Lucie's recipe book at my side. Oysters for all four of us would be a lot of work—all that elbow grease involved in opening them at the last minute. And there's no proper shucking knife in Rose's rather basic holiday kitchen, so I'd need to use a screwdriver or one of the heavy chef's knives that I have, and that would risk mortal injury to my poor hand which has only just recovered from its encounter with the hatchet. I should probably let Doctor Didier have a day off, given that it will be Christmas, so I decide to make discretion the better part of valour and give the oysters a miss on this occasion.

I'll make a beautiful *velouté* instead, seeking inspiration from whatever vegetables are in season in the shops. A warming butternut squash and ginger, perhaps? Then we'll follow it with the sea bream and the duck for the main course, as planned. And, of course, dessert is now the Christmas pudding.

I add everything I'll need to my shopping list. And what about Christmas gifts for my guests? I'll have to seek inspiration in the shops in Sainte-Foy when I get down there.

Pulling on my coat and winding a long woollen muffler around my neck, I pick up my shopping basket and step out into the snowy yard. The snow is deeper than I'd realised from behind the safety of my windows, and the surface is lethally icy, so that my feet nearly slide out from under me, making me lurch most inelegantly and windmill my arms to keep my balance.

I hear Eliane then, calling me as she peers out from the doorway of the barn, and I make my way cautiously across the yard, slipping and sliding as my boots crunch through the snow and meet the treacherous sheet of ice that lurks beneath it.

'*Oh là-là*,' she laments, ushering me into the barn. Its lofty roof rises above our heads, supported on ancient beams that look as if they were hewn from vast tree trunks. In the soft, dusky light within the shelter of the old stone walls, the horse stands patiently in her stall, quietly eating her breakfast. The air is scented with the sundried hay that lies about her in soft drifts, mingling with her warm, animal smell.

'You see, Evie, I told you there was a storm on the way. The birds and the moon are never mistaken. Did you hear how that wind got up again suddenly last night? And for it to have sleeted first, so it froze when it hit the cold ground, and then snowed so heavily on top of it! I've never seen the weather so confused, so *perturbé*. The conditions are lethal.'

I have to confess to having heard none of it. So Eliane's long-awaited storm finally arrived and I slept right through it.

The white mare stomps her feet and shifts around uneasily in the fresh hay that Eliane's strewn round the stall, having just mucked it out judging by the wheelbarrow full of fragrantly damp straw that steams gently in the barn's doorway.

'All right, old lady,' Eliane pats the horse's firm neck. 'Feeling a bit uncomfortable now are you? Never mind, not long to go.'

The mare's flanks do look swollen. 'When's the foal due exactly?' I ask.

'Should be a couple more weeks. Nearly there now. Her friend the owl is keeping an eye on her.'

Eliane picks up the shovel she's been using to muck out the stall and beckons to me to follow her to the back of the barn. In a corner, directly beneath one of the high beams, there's a little heap of pellets on the floor, and a single, beautiful white feather patterned with fine brown spots, which I pick up. Eliane puts a finger to her lips and points upwards. I crane my neck and can just make out the curve of a feathered back, high up in the roof. Eliane scoops up the owl pellets with her shovel and it scrapes slightly on the cement floor. At the sound, a heart-shaped face swivels round to peer down at us, its eyes round and surprised as it surveys these intruders in its domain. We creep back out of the barn, with a final pat for the horse, who nods her head and whinnies softly as we leave. Eliane pushes the barrow of muck round the back and adds it to the manure heap.

'We let this rot and then dig it into the vegetable patch in the spring. Nothing better for enriching the soil.'

I stroke the barn owl's feather, smoothing its perfect pattern of tawny spots on a pure white ground. 'So beautiful.'

Eliane nods. 'That's one of its breast feathers. Its back is brown, as you saw, but underneath its chest is as white as its face, with these little brown markings. We call it a *chouette effraie*, or sometimes a *dame blanche*. Some say they are the souls of the dead who haven't yet left us.'

'A white lady,' I muse. 'Very apt. It does look a bit ghostly when it soars out of the barn and off into the dusk with its wings spread wide.' It's funny to think how terrified I used to be, lying awake in the dark and hearing the owl's screeching cry, when I first arrived. It's part of the soundtrack of my life now: it makes me feel like I belong.

I take the car keys out of my pocket, my mind turning to my shopping expedition, and then catch sight of the expression of horrified incredulity on Eliane's face.

'You're not seriously considering trying to drive your car in this, are you?'

I look a little dubiously at the snow underfoot, shifting my feet gingerly over that treacherous layer of black ice that underlies it.

'Well, I was going to try...'

She grabs my arm with her surprisingly strong grip. 'I absolutely forbid it, Evie. It would be sheer madness. You haven't got chains or snow tyres and, even with those—Didier hasn't risked going out today, look.' She points over to where I can now make out the snowy mound that conceals his car, tucked round the side of his house to leave the garage free for more important things. There aren't any vehicle tracks at all in the snow, now she comes to mention it: not in the yard, not up the driveway, not in front of Eliane's cottage, not on the road. The snow lies undisturbed all around us, a perfect blanket of whiteness, glittering innocently in the sunlight as it conceals the sheer skating rink that lies beneath.

'Oh,' is all I can say, as pennies start to drop; and then the pennies cascade like a Vegas slot machine that's just decided to pay out big time. 'I guess you don't have snowploughs here then?'

She shakes her head. 'On the *autoroutes*, yes. But I'm afraid our steep rural lanes are at the very bottom of the list of priorities. We're so un-used to snow like this. *Ce n'est pas normal.* '

'No gritting trucks?'

'*Non.* And even then, on this ice, the roads would still be impossible. It's a very fast, one-way ticket into the ditch under these conditions. Mathieu won't even risk taking the tractor out today.'

'Oh,' I say again.

'You were just setting off to do your shopping for Christmas?' she surmises.

I nod. 'So now I have no provisions, no gifts, no electricity, no stove—even if I did have any food to cook on it. I do have a cold, three-quarters cooked Christmas pudding though. Sorry, Eliane; it's not exactly the Christmas feast I wanted to give you.'

Because my Christmas menu suddenly looks as though it's going to be:

*Can of baked beans, found in back of Rose's
cupboards. Served cold*

♦

Not-quite-cooked Christmas Pudding. Also served cold.

She shakes her head. '*Oh là-là*, child, you should know better than that. The company is what counts. We're used to occasional storms and power cuts here and when they happen we all rally round. Come, let's go and see what the situation is in your kitchen. Between us, we'll manage to make a Christmas feast fit for a king. Oh, and by the way, our *Réveillon* dinner at Mireille's will most certainly be cancelled. The phones are out, so we have no way of communicating with them, but Mathieu has said there's no way we can get there, not with this ice on the roads. The temperature will plummet at night under these clear skies, making it even more dangerous.'

I nod, now fully accepting that whatever she says goes, as far as weather forecasting is concerned.

'So,' she continues, 'you and Didier will come to us tomorrow evening for a *Réveillon* feast, and then we'll all come to you on Christmas Day. Perfect.'

She sweeps ahead of me across the yard, her sturdy farm boots gripping the ice far better than my more lightweight pair, which leave me slipping and sliding in her wake, like a rather unsteady pageboy following a very regal Good Queen Wenceslas.

'When do you think the power will come back on? Otherwise I have no way of cooking. Surely it'll be back on by tomorrow?'

Eliane shrugs. 'Who knows; it depends how many lines have come down and exactly where they are. We've had outages that have lasted up to a week in the past. I'm afraid that, as with the road, Les Pélérins is usually way down the list of the electricity company's priorities as we're so tiny and so far off the beaten track. But what do you mean, you have no way of cooking? You've got a perfectly good range.'

I've always regarded the antique, wood-fired oven that sits in the corner of the kitchen as just a bit of Rose's quirky decor. Never for a moment did I think it might still be in working order.

'Does it work?' I ask, dubiously.

'It works perfectly! We always make sure the chimney is swept each year along with all the others; it's one of the things we organise for Rose and Max. Though they never use it, of course, because they're only ever here in the summer.'

She crouches in front of the iron belly of the old range, feeding in paper and kindling and showing me how to slide open the air intake to get the fire to blaze brightly at first. 'Then, when you've got the bigger logs burning, you close it a bit, like this'—she demonstrates—'to regulate the heat.'

The whole room already feels more cheerful, with the promise of warmth beginning to pervade the chill that I've gotten used to over the past weeks. Why didn't I think of asking her about the stove before now? It's the perfect way of warming the heart of the house.

'Now, let's see what you have in your cupboards. And then we'll go over to my house and find whatever else you need. I'm looking forward to being cooked for by a proper chef—what a treat!'

An hour later, my Christmas dinner menu has been revised, yet again, so that now it reads as follows:

Cheese gougères with a glass of champagne

◆

Chestnut soup

◆

Roast loin of pork, stuffed with Périgord truffle
Celeriac purée
Roast potatoes
Garnish of fried sage leaves

◆

Christmas Pudding with Cognac butter

Eliane gives it a nod of approval. 'That sounds delicious. I can't wait to try your grandmother's recipe for the pork.'

'I know; it's a good job I forgot to give Didier back the rest of the truffle. It'll be perfect. And everything—with the exception of that tin of chestnuts which was hiding behind the baked beans at the back of one of Rose's cupboards—is from right here.

Mamie Lucie would definitely approve. But what am I going to do about the wines to accompany it? I've got one bottle of champagne, but that's all. It's not exactly going to make it the merriest Christmas ever.'

Eliane looks at me like I'm totally crazy. 'Evie,' she says patiently, 'you live in a vineyard. Mathieu will bring some wines down from the château. I know Henri would be delighted to think he'd helped us out in our Christmas crisis.'

◆ ◆ ◆

As I bustle about my newly cosy kitchen, mixing and peeling, chopping and simmering in the good old-fashioned way, I find myself humming a carol or two and planning to go out and cut some branches of bay and gather some strands of ivy with which to deck the halls. In the words of the song, and despite all resolutions to the contrary, it's beginning to look a lot like Christmas about these parts...

As dusk falls, I survey my day's work. Despite the snow and ice and the lack of electricity, the house is the warmest it's been, with both the fire and the range blazing away merrily. The kitchen is full of delicious aromas of cooking, and I'm now well ahead with my preparations for the day after tomorrow. I've draped ivy and sprigs of red-berried holly around the picture frames in the sitting room and have laid a couple of pine branches along the mantle shelf, from where their needles breathe their Christmas scent into the warm air. Outside, the snow gleams in the fading light, cushioning the windowsills with its soft whiteness.

I place a cream-coloured candle on a saucer, setting it in the window beside the front door—my candle for Lucie—and hold a match to the wick. The flame burns steadily, unwavering.

I've made a wreath of bay and holly for the front door, so I tie a loop of red ribbon onto it, shrug on my jacket, and step out into the yard to hang it. Not bad, even if I do say so myself. The house looks truly festive and welcoming with the green and scarlet wreath, and Lucie's candle burning in the window beside it.

All of a sudden, there's a whoosh of wings and I gasp, ducking and clutching my head involuntarily as the owl swoops out of the barn and flies straight towards me, banking sharply at the last moment. Its screeching call sounds frantic in the still evening air.

How strange.

I stand for a moment, a little shaken, as the pale apparition disappears off into the dusk. I recall, with a shiver, what Eliane said about people believing them to be the souls of the dead.

I shake my head and go to push open the front door and retreat into the reassuring warmth and light of the house, when I hear a muffled thudding noise coming from the barn. And, as I make my way cautiously across the yard, slipping and sliding on the ice, I hear a sound that makes my heart contract with fear. It's a low moan, the sound of an animal in pain.

I reach the stable and peer into the stall. The horse is down in the straw, lying on her side, her distended belly taut. Her eyes roll in her head, which is thrown back, and her soft, velvety muzzle is flecked with foam. Every now and then she kicks her legs, her hooves knocking against the wooden partition. The foal is arriving! But, I wonder desperately, is this normal? She looks terrified; in pain. Surely it's not supposed to be like this?

I run, as fast as my skidding feet can carry me, up the drive and over the road. 'Eliane! Mathieu!' I shout, my voice sounding shrill with panic in the snow-shrouded silence. There's no sign of them, nor of Bruno. I can see footprints in the snow leading off up the hill to the château, or maybe into the woods. I can't risk wasting time going up there to look for them when they could be anywhere, in the wine cellar, visiting the graveyard, hunting in the woods...

From the barn across the road, I hear another deep groan of pain from the mare.

I skid back down the drive and hammer on Didier's door. He emerges, raking his fingers through his hair, his smile turning to a look of concern at the expression on my face.

I gasp, 'Didier, please, come quick. It's the horse. There's something wrong...'

By the time we arrive back in the stable, she's kicked the straw around her away, her legs flailing with her struggle. Didier takes a look, assessing.

'I don't know much about horses, but I do know that when things go wrong it's usually *really* bad news. Quick, Evie, let's try and get her up on her feet. From the look of things, I'm guessing perhaps the placenta is misplaced and it's blocking the foal's exit. We need to get her moving, to try and get it to shift.' His voice is calm and low, but I sense the note of underlying urgency.

Trembling all over, I come to kneel at the horse's head. Her rolling eyes focus on me as I lay a hand on her smooth neck. It feels hot, moist with sweat.

'Okay, old girl. It's going to be okay.' I hope I sound less afraid than I feel.

She raises her head, just a little, at the sound of my voice, perhaps recognising the friend who's brought her a daily apple.

'That's good,' Didier says. 'Try to reassure her. Keep talking to her. I'll come round and push from the other side.'

The mare's legs flail again, her flanks heaving as she gasps in a breath and then groans, a harrowing sound that seems to come from deep in her belly.

'Okay now, help her lift her head as I push against her shoulder here.'

She's weak, exhausted with her efforts, but as we help her she tries to gather her legs beneath her; rises a little; then collapses back onto the floor.

'Again!' Didier's voice is more urgent now. 'Lift her head!'

'Come on!' I plead with her, 'Get up. Try! We'll help you, please just try once more!'

With a surge of desperation, she draws her legs inwards and, somehow, miraculously, heaves herself up.

'Oh, thank God!'

'Don't let her fall, support her head. We need to try and get her to walk.' Didier encourages her, tugging on the coarse strands of her mane, and she staggers forwards a step or two.

'That's good, keep her moving,' he urges, and we circle the stable, each with a hand on her neck, her steps becoming steadier and her gasping, shallow breaths deepening a little, plumes of steam puffing into the night air.

Is it my imagination, or does the brutal hardness of her belly seem to release slightly?

'It's working!' I cry. 'Didier, I think it's working!'

'Keep moving.' We walk her round and round, her hooves clomping on the straw-strewn cement.

And then she nods her head up and down three times. An affirmation? Her way of saying she can handle it from here? Because she stops in her tracks, drops her head and then sinks down onto her knees, lowering herself to the floor. There's a gush of liquid, and then suddenly, with a heave and a slither, her foal is born. It's wrapped in a sac of tissue but, with a toss of its head, it breaks free and emerges into the world, gasping its first breath into its newborn body, the colour of black velvet, a single white star emblazoned on its forehead.

Hot tears of relief and gratitude flood into my eyes.

Didier stands back, a broad smile spreading across his face. And, without thinking, I step towards him and he opens his arms and pulls me in, holding me tight against his body.

The mare looks round, turning towards her baby, lying with her muzzle close to the foal's head.

'What do we do now?' I whisper.

'Nothing,' Didier's eyes glint in the moonlit darkness of the barn, his arm still encircling my waist. 'We let nature take its course. She will deliver the afterbirth in a while. But look, she knows what to do.'

The mare pulls herself to her feet and gently touches her foal's head with her nose, then begins to clean her baby. We creep out into the yard, leaving the pair in peace for a few moments.

The moon is just beginning to rise, no longer rust-coloured now, but a luminous silver, its rays streaming through the doorway of the barn to illuminate the nativity scene within. 'Look.' I point to a star, bigger than any of the others, that hangs in the sky just above the barn roof. 'Our very own Christmas star! Hanging above the stable like a sign. Perhaps they'll name the foal "Star". Or "Noël".'

'"Jupiter" might be more appropriate,' Didier smiles. 'That star is a planet.'

We stand close together, underneath the oaks, as the Milky Way drapes itself across the universe above us, illuminating the dark sky with the most beautiful show of Christmas lights imaginable.

Didier takes both my hands in his. 'Well done, Evie; that mare and her foal would almost certainly have died if it weren't for you.'

'Actually it was thanks to the owl. And you too. Let's call it a team effort. But I don't know where Eliane and Mathieu have got to. We'd better go find them and tell them what's happened.'

He nods. 'In a minute. They told me they were going to the woods to catch rabbits for our *Réveillon* dinner tomorrow. They called earlier, to invite me to join you all.' And then he looks down at me and his smile fades, the look on his face both serious and tender suddenly. '*Réveillon*,' he muses. 'How apt that word is.'

'The French word for Christmas Eve? Why, what does it mean?'

'We use it to mean "staying awake", because originally it used to signify the meal eaten when people came home from midnight mass. But I think this year I prefer its more literal meaning. It comes from the word that means a reawakening. *Se réveiller*.'

I nod slowly, taking this in.

'You and I have both been hibernating, Evie, through the very long and very cold winter of our grief. But now, I sense it's time for us to reawaken. To re-enter the world. Reborn, like that little fellow in the barn. You know, Christmas used to be my worst time of the year. But *this* year I think it's going to be different.'

'You're right,' I whisper. 'It's taken coming here, to get away from it all, to remind me what Christmas is truly all about.'

I look across the yard to where Lucie's candle burns steadily in the window.

Didier notices. And he must guess the significance of the tiny flame that shines out into the darkness. He hesitates a moment. Then asks, 'When you lost your baby, Evie, did they do any tests to try to find out why?'

It's still painful to think about that time, the hospital sheets cold and stiff, lying there with my heart shattering into a thousand pieces as the nurse came and gently took Lucie from my arms, carrying her away from me forever.

'The doctor said they couldn't be sure, but it might have been a problem with the placenta.' My voice is low, the words hard to say. 'Perhaps it didn't develop properly. She didn't get enough nutrients. In the end, her heart just stopped. It must have been my fault I guess. Feeling so sick; not eating properly.'

He squeezes my hands tightly. 'No, Evie. You do know, don't you, that there's no way it's your fault? And that it's unlikely that the same thing should happen if you decide to try again? Did they tell you that?'

'I'm too scared,' I whisper. 'It would be too much of a risk.'

I raise my eyes to his and his expression is tender. 'Scared? No, Evie, not you. You have immense courage. Look how calm you were this evening. Look how brave you've been, coming to this strange place, where you know no one. Look at all the love you have in your heart. The love you have for life.'

I shrug. 'Sometimes life seems to be very fragile.' I incline my head towards the barn. 'That happy ending there could easily have been a tragedy instead.'

'Yes, but it wasn't. We took a risk. We used our instincts. And in the end, life won. I've seen enough of this world to know that if there's one thing worth taking a risk on, it's life. I hope you will have children of your own, because you will be a wonderful mother, Evie.'

'How do you know? No one can know that. What if I'm not? Or what if I fail again?'

'I know because I can see how much you loved your baby, your Lucie. It's because you loved her so much that you are hurting so much now. You know, they say that grief is the price we pay for love. But, no matter how much it hurts, it's always a price worth paying. And so we have to be brave enough to take a risk, even when we've been hurt more than we can bear, we have to find the courage to put our hearts on the line again for love's sake. Sometimes it takes years to be able to do so, but you will get there in the end. I never imagined I'd be able to find that courage, that strength, again, but now, somehow, with you...' He tails off.

I nod slowly. I understand that he's not just talking about my grief, but about his own as well. That he feels, as I do, that tonight something wonderful has happened. The miracle of the foal's birth had brought us even closer, shown us that, together, we can give one another the courage to take risks again. And maybe, even, take the biggest risk of all: to love again, wholeheartedly.

He smiles down at me, his eyes bright in the starlight. 'I know it's a paradox, Evie, but it's your grief and your pain that prove what a great mother you will be. You have so much love to give, and yes, you're right, nothing is ever assured in this world. But whether it's in loving your own children, or children you might adopt, or your nephews and nieces, or godchildren... there are very many ways to fulfil that love.'

Distracted suddenly, he glances towards Eliane's cottage. 'Look, I think they're coming back, there's torchlight on the road. I'll go and tell them.'

I creep back into the barn. In the moonlight, the mare stands with her head bowed, almost touching her foal's neck. His white blaze gleams in the moonlight and his legs are out-splayed, all awkward angles; but, as I watch, he tries to stand, wobbling and then collapsing back down in a heap of long-limbed cuteness. His mother watches over him, tenderly protective, patiently waiting for him to gather the strength to try again. She turns her head to look at me as I lean over the stable door. And, as we hear the voices of the others enter the yard, she nods once again and gives a soft, low whinny of contentment.

'Good girl,' I murmur. 'What a good mother you are.' And I remember Didier's words and think, *maybe one day. Just maybe.*

Later, as I'm about to get into bed, I reach under the bedstead and haul out my suitcase. When I arrived here, I unpacked and stowed my belongings into the closet and the dresser that stand pushed back against the whitewashed walls of the bedroom. Everything except one last item. I take out the sealed envelope now, sitting on the floor with my back against the bed frame. It hasn't been opened since the midwife handed it to me as we left the hospital. 'They're in here,' she said to me, her smile kind. 'In case, you know, one day...'

I haven't had the courage to open it before now. I hesitate for a moment, then carefully ease up the flap.

Three photographs fall into my lap. A close-up of Lucie, swaddled in a pink, honeycombed receiving blanket, a wisp of strawberry blonde hair, fine as thistledown, just visible above her closed eyes. A photo of me, leaning back against a pile of snowy hospital pillows, cradling her in my arms. And a close-up of two hands, one with breathtakingly tiny, perfect fingers that curl softly in my larger, more lined palm.

I sit and look at them for a long, long time until I'm ready to unfurl my stiffened legs and clamber into bed, placing the pictures carefully on the nightstand.

Keeping them close to me, all through the night.

Chapter 9
Bring a torch, Jeannette, Isabelle

Bring a torch, Jeannette, Isabelle!
Bring a torch, to the cradle run...

After so many weeks, it feels kind of weird to be putting on anything other than my usual outfit of jeans, thick socks and several layers of sweaters, but I'm making an effort as it's *Réveillon* and it's fun having an excuse to get dressed up for once. So, even though it'll just be the four of us—comprising, as we do, the sum total of the population of the hamlet of Les Pélerins—I've soaked in a hot bath, slicked on a little eyeliner and lip colour, and smoothed my newly washed hair into a glossy chignon that glints with copper lights in the bathroom mirror as I tuck in the last couple of bobby-pins to hold an unruly tendril or two in place. I'm wearing the one skirt I brought with me, with a cream silk blouse, and I ease on a pair of drop-pearl earrings.

There's a knock at the front door and I race downstairs to open it to Didier, looking more handsome than ever in a shirt and sports jacket. He steps in out of the cold and kisses me on both cheeks. '*Bonsoir,* Madame Evie. How very elegant you look tonight.'

'*Merci,* Doctor Didier, and I could say the same for you! Now, hold that thought for just a moment...' I ruin the effect by shrugging on my thick coat and pushing my feet into a pair of rubber boots that I'll wear to shuffle up the drive and across the road to Mathieu and Eliane's cottage, because the snow still lies thick on the ground with that treacherous sheet of ice lurking beneath it. Given my track record in front of Didier, I'm not risking any more bruises on my behind this evening.

I pick up the bag that contains my high-heeled shoes, which I'll swap once I'm safely inside, and gather up the bay wreath that I've made as a *Réveillon* gift for my hosts. I've had to be creative in the absence of any chance of a shopping expedition, but I'm quite pleased with my efforts. I cut branches from the bay tree that grows on one side of the terrace, shaking off the snow and choosing sprigs with as many bayberries as possible, then wired them into a circle and added cinnamon sticks and star anise here and there, plundered from Rose's store cupboard, tying it with a broad cream grosgrain ribbon. It's both decorative and practical, and I hope Eliane will hang it in her kitchen and slowly dismantle it through the months to come as she uses its component parts to flavour her cooking.

Didier chivalrously offers me his arm and I take it—well, the conditions underfoot really are awfully slippery, that's why—and we proceed, with cautious steps, towards the welcoming glow of the lights that shine out across the snow from the windows of the cottage. The night is perfectly still and clear, the smoke rising straight up from the chimney stack and clouding the stars above the roof with its soft, sweet-scented mist that reminds me of wood fires back home.

Bruno greets us at the gate, his tail wagging enthusiastically, and lets out a short bark or two to announce our arrival. Mathieu throws open the door and welcomes us in. The greetings over, we all stand in front of the fire in the sitting room, awkward for a moment, our unaccustomed finery making us feel a little self-conscious, until Eliane bustles through from the kitchen, pulling off her apron and smoothing her fine white hair into place. 'Come, Mathieu, aperitifs for our guests!'

Each with a generous glass of Kir, the blackcurrant liqueur adding a rosy hint of festivity to the dry white

Bordeaux wine, the conversation begins to flow and soon we're laughing and chatting as Eliane hands round a plate of little wild mushroom tartlets to accompany the drinks. I'm impressed that she has managed to conjure something so delicious out of thin air.

Outside, the darkness is suddenly disturbed by a gust of gruff barking.

'Bruno! *Tais-toi!*' shouts Mathieu. And as Bruno falls quiet, we stare at one another in amazement.

Because, through the silent night beyond the cottage walls, comes the sound of angelic voices, raised in song.

'What on earth...?' exclaims Eliane. 'I don't believe it!'

She throws open the front door and we step out into the snow. And there, coming up the road, is an astonishing sight.

First come several girls, ranging in age from about twelve to their late teens, carrying torches that light the way for a woman of about my age, accompanied by a teenage boy, who are pulling a sledge on which sits a bright-eyed toddler, tightly wrapped in cosy layers like a papoose. They're all singing a French carol, which I recognise from my Paris days. '*Un flambeau, Jeannette, Isabelle—Un flambeau! Courons au berceau!*' 'Bring a torch, Jeannette, Isabelle, bring a torch, to the cradle run...' Their voices, clear as a carillon of Christmas bells, float up to us on the frosty air, and we laugh aloud when they get to the second verse, waving their torches in greeting...

> *'Who goes there, knocking on the door?*
> *Who goes there, knocking like that?*
> *Open up, I've arranged on a platter*
> *Delicious cakes, which I've brought here.*
> *Knock! Knock! Knock! Open the door for us!*
> *Knock! Knock! Knock! Let's celebrate!'*

Behind them, a large truck is reversing slowly up the road with its tailgate down and from the back several lusty young men are shovelling grit onto the snow-covered lane so that the truck's chain-clad wheels can grip safely. And, bringing up the rear of this unlikely procession, is a blue pickup truck, whose headlights are helping to illuminate the whole scene.

Eliane brings her hands to her cheeks, laughing and crying all at once. 'It's Nathalie! And Hélène! And Héloise! Oh, and Gina and Luc, with little Pierre on the sled! I don't believe it! And all the boys...'

Mathieu hugs her to him with a burly arm. 'A *Réveillon* miracle, *hein,* old lady? Trust the family to find a way for us to spend it all together!'

He and Didier go out into the lane to help the carol singers pull the sled the last few yards up to the cottage and suddenly the little house is full of noise and laughter and bustle as they come, stamping the snow from their boots, pulling off jackets and gloves, crowding round Eliane and Mathieu to kiss them and hug them.

The blue pickup has pulled up right before the gate and another man gets out of the driver's cab and comes round to help the last passenger out, a little old lady with a walking stick. Flanked by two of the sturdy young men, she is carefully escorted up the path until at last she stands in front of Eliane.

'Mireille! How wonderful. You all came! All of you!' Eliane can hardly speak for the tears of joy that are running down her cheeks.

'But of course. You didn't think we'd leave you alone at *Réveillon*, did you, my dear sister? I've made enough venison à la Bordelaise to feed an army, knowing that it's Mathieu's favourite dish,' she pauses to pinch his rosy cheeks and the old man blushes and beams at her in adoration, 'and the boys managed to get down to the town this morning and bought about a ton of oysters. Raphael's been shucking them all afternoon. I'm glad to see you've got company,' she turns and nods regally to Didier and me, as we stand to one side to allow the family time to exchange their greetings, 'because we're going to need all the help we can get!'

Eliane wipes her eyes, pulling herself together, beaming now. 'Evie, Didier, let me introduce you to the entire Thibault clan, who are crazy enough to brave the ice and snow to bring us a proper *Réveillon* dinner!'

I struggle to keep track of all the names as the family file past, one by one, and we exchange countless kisses. As far as I can work it out, in all the confusion of noise and laughter, Mireille has four sons, Raphael, Florian, Cédric, and Pierre. Raphael's pretty twin daughters, Hélène and Héloise, home from university for the holidays, and Cédric's daughter, Nathalie, are the carol singers. Gina and Luc, who were pulling the toddler—*le petit Pierre*, as everyone calls him—on the sled, are Cédric's wife and son; Florian and his wife Marie-Louise are the parents of three of the sturdy young men who were shovelling the grit from the back of the truck, driven up here by their father; and then there are three more men who were also involved in the shovelling: two are the grown-up sons of Raphael and the other is their uncle, Mireille's youngest son, also called Pierre.

Mireille directs the wives of her three eldest sons to bring in pots and trays of food from the back of the pickup and then she and Eliane supervise the arrangement of these on a big trestle table, hastily put up in the kitchen by Mathieu and Didier and covered with a clean white tablecloth. Eliane uses my wreath as a centrepiece, lighting candles to flank it, and I help Gina set out cutlery, plates and glasses, as the noise levels reach a crescendo in the little cottage. Chairs are fetched and bottles of wine are opened and offered around by Florian and Cédric, and in and out of this flurry of activity the younger children scamper and giggle, delighted at their adventurous journey through the arctic landscape to get here, and the excitement of this impromptu party.

Once everyone is settled around the long table, Raphael's twins circulate with vast platters on which the oysters are displayed, bedecked with seaweed and lemon quarters. We each pile a few onto our plates— even little Pierre is given a couple, which he eats with gusto—and soon there's nothing left but heaps of empty shells.

'*Délicieux*. Worth all the hard work,' pronounces Raphael, displaying a bandaged thumb as proof of the hazards involved in opening the oysters' tight-clamped shells.

The two elderly sisters, Eliane and Mireille, sit side by side at the top of the table. Eliane shakes her head, still hardly able to believe she has her beloved family around her. 'How on earth did you manage to get into town today? And, which was even more impossible, how on earth did you manage to get here tonight?'

Cédric, who is pulling the corks from bottles of red wine to accompany the main course, pauses in his work and grins at his aunt. 'I'll give you three guesses! You know it would take more than the storm of the century to keep your big sister from getting the entire family together on Christmas Eve. First of all, she telephoned the Mayor and told him that if he could get a load of grit delivered from the regional depot in Libourne then she would volunteer her sons and grandsons to come with the truck and help grit the roads of the *commune*. On one small condition, though: that we be allowed to keep back just enough for gritting the lane to Les Pélérins as well. Then she sent Raphael off down to Sainte-Foy—where luckily the main road has been ploughed clear—risking life and limb for our *Réveillon* oysters.'

His son, Luc, chips in eagerly, 'Yes, and then tonight we came along the top of the escarpment to get here, gritting the road along the way. I helped shovel too, didn't I *Papa*?'

'You did indeed, *mon fils*.' Cédric ruffles his elder son's hair fondly.

Mireille smiles serenely, nodding her approval as Marie-Louise brings a fragrantly steaming casserole of venison stew to the table and sets it down in front of her mother-in-law so that she can spoon helpings onto the plates that are passed up to her. 'We parcelled up the meal and brought it in the back of the pickup. Here,' she passes me a dish of mashed potatoes, 'help yourself, there's plenty.'

I turn to Florian, who's sitting on my left. 'So what do you do when you're not being press-ganged into gritting the roads for the local community?'

He laughs. 'In our day jobs, we work as stonemasons. Hence the truck. But our mother likes to deploy us wherever she thinks we're needed most.' He beams fondly at Mireille as she directs operations from the head of the table.

'Fortunately for me,' chips in Gina, who's sitting on the other side of me. To my great delight, I've discovered she's English, although her French is so good that I mistook her for a local at first. 'Mireille took it upon herself to deploy her sons to come to my rescue in the aftermath of a summer storm. That's how I met Cédric.'

'Ah, yes, God works in mysterious ways,' her husband says, raising his glass in a toast to his mother and Eliane.

'He does indeed,' Mireille raises her glass in turn. 'Sometimes He just needs a little helping hand though!'

Eliane shakes her head, smiling. 'My dear sister, even if you hadn't got involved, Gina and Cédric would most certainly have ended up together. It was their Fate. And, no matter what we humans do to mess things up, Fate has a way of working it all out in the end.'

Cédric reaches for Gina's hand and laces his fingers through hers. 'Well, call it Fate or call it Family— thank goodness for happy endings!'

At that, prompted by Raphael, we all raise our glasses together in a toast. 'To happy endings,' we chorus.

I look around the crowded table, content to sit quietly for a moment as the sea of family chatter continues to ebb and flow, watching Eliane's face as she presides over the unexpected *Réveillon* gathering. Her expression is one of pure joy, and written into it is a love so strong, so wholehearted, that it gives me hope. Just for a moment, in the midst of all that noise and light and warmth, I spare a thought for the little graveyard up the hill. For Eliane's babies. For Mathieu's father and brother, killed in the war. Looking at my hosts' faces this evening, I see unfeigned happiness. And so much love. There are no traces of the shadows that I myself feel, of anger, fear and grief. *So this is where forgiveness leads*, I think. To open-hearted, full-on joy. It feels like a gift, given to me by Eliane and Mathieu. Showing me that they truly *are* living their lives on behalf of the ones they've lost. A way to be... My future.

Didier has been commandeered by Mireille and seated between her and one of the twins—Hélène I think it is. But as I look around the table, savouring my meal and quietly basking in the sunshine of the family's love and laughter, he glances my way. Catching my eye, he smiles and raises his glass just a fraction of an inch, in a private toast of our own. I wonder whether he's feeling what I'm feeling, that this truly is a *Réveillon* celebration in the literal sense of the word: a reawakening of the soul; a re-entry into life.

I think perhaps Gina notices our exchanged glance, because she nudges me and says, 'Our Doctor Didier is a very popular addition to the community. We just hope he's going to stay on. If only there were something to help keep him here... But I suspect Africa is calling him back. And you, how long are you planning on staying, Evie?'

'Oh, probably just until the New Year. Then I shall need to get back to work. I'll definitely be going back to the States in February for the arrival of my sister's baby. I guess that'll be a good opportunity to take a look around, think about my future. Maybe I'll scout for premises for a small restaurant in the Boston area. Working with Eliane in the garden and the kitchen has fired my enthusiasm for cooking again. I'd like to adapt my grandmother's recipes to give them a modern twist, and use them as the basis for the menu. I might even compile them into a recipe book—I'm thinking of calling it something like *Sensational Seasonal Cooking*!'

'Ooh, that's a great idea!'

'What is?' chips in Cédric, stooping between us and holding a platter of interesting-looking cheeses steady for Gina. She helps herself to several different slivers and then hands me the knife so that I can follow suit.

'Make sure you take a slice of the *Trappe d'Echourgnac*. It's a local cheese, cured in a walnut liqueur. The taste is amazing.' She turns to her husband. 'Evie's going to write a cookbook taking traditional French recipes and adding a modern twist to them *Génial, n'est-ce pas?*

Didier overhears. 'Well, I can vouch for the fact that she's an excellent cook.'

Eliane nods. 'She knows how to get the very best out of whatever's available too. I'm already looking forward to our Christmas lunch tomorrow!'

Mireille fixes me with her bright-eyed gaze. 'Good for you, Evie. But, you know, these days so many people have forgotten how to cook. They think pre-paring a meal involves putting a plastic pot into the microwave for five minutes. You should run cookery courses too, showing people what can be done with simple, fresh ingredients and a little imagination.'

'That's brilliant, Mireille,' Gina's face lights up with enthusiasm as the idea begins to gather momentum. 'And I know just the venue for the courses...'

'Of course! Château Bellevue. She could run courses there in the winter, when they're not busy with weddings. You must introduce Evie to Sara and Thomas, Gina.'

'They've got the accommodation, and a huge kitchen. And it's such a beautiful setting. What do you think, Hélène? Héloise? The twins work there in the summer, you see,' Gina explains in an aside to me.

'It could work, yes; it would be wonderful. It would extend the season for them. And cookery courses would be much simpler to organise than the weddings are...'

I pop a morsel of the walnut-flavoured cheese into my mouth. Gina's right; it's delicious, a combination I've never come across before. I nod slowly, mulling over the idea, the general enthusiasm for it around the table helping fire up my own sense of inspiration. 'Sounds great. In fact, better than that, it sounds totally brilliant!'

'And Gina, you could present a session on wine tasting as well,' suggests Cédric.

'Even better,' I beam at her. 'We could include wine tasting and suggestions for wine pairings with the different dishes. I'm sure I could get a lot of people from London interested. Maybe even from the States as well. A cookery course like that, set in a lovely French château... what a wonderful experience.'

Didier raises his glass, calling for a moment's silence. 'I'd like to propose another toast: to our enterprising women. The three generations seated at this *Réveillon* table have used the opportunity for a brainstorming session and come up with what sounds like a winning business plan. Here's to them all!'

'Thank you, all of you,' I raise my glass in return. And all at once there's such a lump in my throat that I have to swallow before I can speak. 'Thank you for your friendship and your enthusiasm, as well as for including me in your family party.' I can't say any more, because the word 'family' has made sudden tears prick my eyes. So I take another fortifying sip of the rich red wine to allow the surge of emotions within me to pass.

Sensing that I'm a little overwhelmed, Gina puts an arm around my shoulders and makes a toast of her own: 'To friendships, old and new!'

The others echo her, their words reverberating round the room, and seeming to amplify the warmth and light within this little cottage nestling in the snowy countryside.

'And now,' Mireille claps her hands, 'the dessert!'

Hélène and Héloïse carry in a tray, on which sits the biggest and finest *Bûche de Noël* I've ever seen, and everyone bursts out laughing as little Pierre, who has been leaning his sleepy head against his father's shoulder, suddenly sits up straight, his eyes growing wide with delight at the sight of so much chocolate cake. 'Well, that's certainly woken you up,' grins Cédric, fondly ruffling his son's fine, dark hair.

Mireille cuts generous slices of the log-shaped roulade, an airy sponge cake which has been rolled up with a rich chocolate mousse. It's as delicious as it looks, covered with a hazelnut praline that adds a satisfying crunch to the soft textures within.

The cacophony of chatter and laughter falls silent for a few moments as everyone savours the dessert. I look up from my plate. 'My grandmother always used to say that the best praise for a dish is a silence just like this one... I wonder, Mireille, would you and Eliane agree to be consultants on my cookbook?' I ask.

Eliane beams, and Mireille nods regally. 'With pleasure, my child.'

And I guess it's all that wine and good food, along-side the company and the fact that it's Christmas Eve, but I feel inordinately pleased to be called 'my child' by this wise woman, and to feel—just for a moment—truly a part of this sprawling, French sur-rogate family.

'So tell us, *Tante* Eliane, will Evie's cookbook be a success?' Raphael asks.

Gina leans towards me, conspiratorially. 'Eliane has a knack for seeing the future. It's uncanny, but quite a few of the things she sees really do seem to come to pass.'

Eliane is gazing at me from the end of the table, and I have the impression, once again, that her grey eyes are focused on things the rest of us cannot see. She smiles at me. 'When Evie spreads her wings, she will achieve many things. She'll go far from us, but she'll still return often too. She has roots here now.'

Mireille nods emphatically. 'That's right. As parents, we try to give our children two things: strong roots, to give them a sense of belonging, and wide wings, to let them fly when the time comes. Maybe your stay here has given you back those things, at a time when your roots had been torn up and your wings broken.'

I drop my eyes to my dessert plate to hide the tears that well up suddenly. Because she's right. I miss my mom and dad and Tess and I know I need to go home to them, back where I belong. But I'm also glad that I have found this place and these people. As Eliane says, I have some roots here now too and I know I'll be back, whatever else the future may hold.

'Well, that's good news for us, that you'll be coming back often,' Gina smiles, kindly giving me a moment to regain my composure. 'Sounds like things are about to take off for you. If your cookbook has both Eliane's and Mireille's seals of approval, it's sure to be a success!'

'And what could be better?' Mireille says. 'Preparing beautiful food is nourishment for mind, body and soul. And then sharing it is a wonderful way of expressing the love that's in your heart, nourishing others.'

Little Pierre looks up from where he's in danger of scraping the pattern off his dessert plate as he scoops up the very last delicious crumbs of the *bûche de Noël*, carefully licking his spoon and relishing the final smidgen of chocolate mousse. 'In that case I think *Mamie* must love us all very, very much,' he announces, and we all burst out laughing at this serious, and heartfelt, pronouncement.

◆ ◆ ◆

'*Au revoir! A bientôt!*' Our farewells ring out through the cold night air accompanied by puffs of white breath, as the brothers carefully help Mireille down the path and back into Cédric's pickup. Gina wraps a warm muffler round her tiny son's neck and helps him pull on a pair of woollen mittens, ready for his sled ride back to the car at the end of the lane. The only features visible are his little button nose and his dark eyes, shining with excitement at this late-night Christmas adventure, as his big brother, Luc, settles him safely into the waiting arms of his sister, Nathalie, who is going to ride on the sled with him.

'Here's my number,' Gina hands me a slip of paper. 'Come and visit us once the snow has melted?'

'I'd love to.' I hug her, delighted to have found a new friend. Actually, I think I've found twenty new friends tonight, but Gina is an especially kindred spirit.

Didier and I say our thank yous and goodnights to Eliane and Mathieu. 'See you tomorrow, around one p.m.,' I confirm.

He offers me a steadying hand as we make our way from the grit-covered roadway onto the more treacherous snow and ice of the driveway. We peer, briefly, into the barn as we pass, and the white horse gives us a quiet snort of recognition as she stands watch over her foal, sleeping soundly in his nest of sweet hay.

We stop beneath one of the tall oaks.

'What an evening!' I throw back my head to look up at the kaleidoscope of stars above us, tipsy on company and warmth, good food and more laughter than I've heard in a long, long time.

'*C'était g*énial! Such a wonderful surprise for Eliane, being able to spend *Réveillon* with her family after all.'

'Did you miss your own family tonight? Being there with all of them?'

He nods. 'Yes, I did. It was a good reminder of what this time of year should really be about. But I think Mireille was right in her remarks about roots and wings. I think you and I have both been damaged, in our different ways, and it's taken time, in this safe refuge, to heal. Being surrounded by people who care has helped me too. It's funny, I came here as their doctor to help them and heal them, and in fact they've ended up being the ones who've helped me to heal. And you, Evie?' he smiles. I realise, all of a sudden, that he's still holding my hand. 'I think I saw from your expression, once or twice tonight, that you were missing your family?'

'I have to admit, I did a little. But it's okay. You're right; I guess we both needed a little space this year, to heal. And, from a distance, it's easier to see things in perspective. Perhaps we have to go away so that we know where we want to get back to. This evening has helped me see that I need to go home. Back to the States. Give these roots a chance to fix themselves.'

I work out the time difference between here and Boston. My family will be just sitting down to eat their own Christmas Eve dinner. Mom usually makes a New England seafood pot pie, a family tradition and one of the few dishes she actually makes from scratch; she'll have stirred a splash of white wine into the sauce, along with clam juice and heavy cream, crammed it full of chunky fresh fish and succulent prawns, then tucked it up under a coverlet of pastry that'll have been baked to a golden crispness. The table will be set with a white lace cloth and candles, and the light will glint softly on the tinsel strands that garland the Christmas tree sitting in the corner of the room. I think of Mireille's words: *preparing beautiful food is nourishment for mind, body and soul. And then sharing it is a wonderful way of expressing the love that's in your heart, nourishing others...* A mother's love.

On the still night air, floating up from the valley below and gently calling my attention back to the here and now, the faint sound of church bells rings out, peal upon peal, the notes soft but clear.

'Sounds like Midnight Mass is over. It's officially Christmas now. Our *Réveillon* vigil is complete.' Didier squeezes my hand but then, instead of letting it go, he takes the other one in his too.

The waning moon bathes us in her soft light. I look into Didier's eyes, as clear as a blue winter sky and, for a moment, as the last peal of bells fades away into silence, the whole world holds its breath again. His expression is unutterably tender, and I wonder if he sees written on my face the same things I see written on his: a landscape, the features given us by our parents and yet unique to ourselves, weathered by pain and grief and joy and love, just as the land around us has been shaped by the wind and rain, and the snow and ice, but by the sunshine too. The landscape of our lives, carved through by a strong-flowing river as it makes its journey from the high heartlands to the infinite ocean beyond the far horizon.

He breaks the spell by glancing upwards, raising his eyebrows quizzically towards the ball of mistletoe that hangs just above our heads in the lowest branches of the tree.

His question, unspoken.

'So, here we are, Evie, two refugees from Christmas who find themselves standing beneath the mistletoe on a perfect snowy night, in front of a stable where a newborn baby lies quietly sleeping, watched over by his mother.' His voice is a whisper, loath to disturb the peace which seems to have settled over the land. Or maybe the peace is just in our formerly troubled hearts as they begin to heal at last, a quiet reawakening after a long winter's hibernation.

I follow his glance, in my turn, and then smile. 'Our own private Christmas story,' I whisper back. And I lean into the warmth of his body.

My unspoken reply.

And so, in the perfect stillness of that Christmas Eve, while the rest of the world sleeps, two souls finally reawaken after a long, cold winter and find the gift of strength, to open their hearts and love again.

Chapter 10
Love Came Down at Christmas

Love came down at Christmas,
Love all lovely, Love Divine...

I awaken to sunlight which floods my bedroom, and lie for a moment, trying to work out what's different about today. And then I remember: everything's different.

It's Christmas morning; the snow has melted off the skylight window, letting the sun shine in; and last night I kissed Didier underneath the starlit mistletoe, falling more deeply in love, in that moment, than I have ever done before.

Of course, in the bright light of day there are all kinds of ifs and buts and how-on-earths about what comes next. Real life, as usual, is complicated. But, you know what? Just for today, I don't care. Today—Christmas Day—is going to be spent with Didier, and our friends Eliane and Mathieu of course, nourishing our newfound love. And whatever comes next, we will deal with it as it arises. Because I know we have the strength to do so. We have deep roots and wide wings, given us by our families and our friends, and so anything is possible.

Stretching my limbs under the luxurious warmth of the bedcovers, I run through in my mind all that I need to do this morning. I'll stoke the fires, carrying in a good supply of logs to warm the house, then I'll set the Christmas pudding on the range for its final boiling; the loin of pork, which I've rolled around fine shavings of rich, earthy truffle, will go into the oven later on; I'll prep the vegetables and I'll set my Christmas table so that all is ready for my guests. And then, at noon here so that they'll just be getting up in Boston, I'll climb the hill to call my family and wish them Merry Christmas.

Hearing the clarion call from the rooster across the lane, I jump out of bed, newfound energy fizzing in my veins, and sing as I make my morning coffee, setting a saucepan of water on the range to boil. '... All I want for Christmas is you!' From the top of the apple tree, the robin cocks his head and bows and dips, joining in with his own version of the chorus. The sunlight makes the ribbons of snow along the branches sparkle as they drop soft drips onto the slowly thawing ground below.

A few hours later I stand, hands on hips, and survey my morning's handiwork. The house is full of warmth, a fire blazing merrily in the sitting room and the range well-stoked, and the low December sun streams in through the window panes of the French doors. Good smells percolate from the kitchen, the roasting meat just starting to crackle in the oven, adding its truffled perfume to the sweetly spiced scent of the pudding which hums merrily to itself from its simmering pan.

Suddenly there's a faint click from the electric cooker, and its digital clock, dead for days since the storm, flashes on. The refrigerator hums back into life. So we even have power back! A Christmas miracle. Not that I need it. The old range is doing its job well and it adds heart to the home with its iron bulk radiating a steady warmth. But I plug my phone in to give it a little extra charge in preparation for my visit to the office up the hill.

I spread a crisp white bed-sheet over the kitchen table in lieu of a suitably Christmassy tablecloth, as all Rose's are covered with prints more suited to summer dining al fresco. I take down a few pretty teacups and saucers from the dresser and put little candles in them, setting them in a circle in the centre of the table and weaving glossy-leaved ivy about them to form a centrepiece. Red linen napkins add a suitably festive touch and the glassware sparkles and winks in the sunlight.

I check my watch—the timing of the cooking all looks fine—and pull on my coat and rubber boots. Just before I open the door, there's one more thing I need to do. I strike a match and hold the flame to the candle on the windowsill. Lucie's candle. So that it'll be shining there to welcome me back on my return from the top of the hill.

I grab my phone, and a couple of carrots that I've kept back, and step out to cross the yard and give the mare a Christmas treat on my way past. The foal, standing more steadily now on legs that still look breath-catchingly fragile, peeps out shyly from behind his mother as she crunches the carrots appreciatively. His white star glows in the soft rays of sunshine that filter in through the barn door, seeming to shine of its own accord.

The snow is melting steadily, and my boots grip the road more easily as I walk up the hill, following once more in the footsteps of a thousand pilgrims who've passed that way before me. I perch on the milestone, surveying the view for a moment and catching my breath. The hollows of the hills, where the sun hasn't quite managed to reach, are still cushioned with blue-shadowed drifts of snow, but the landscape is starting to become green again, damp and newly washed by the thaw. Far off, the church bell chimes twelve times.

I call Rose first, to wish my friend a happy Christmas. 'You sound good, Evie,' she says, after I've filled her in on last night's impromptu dinner party and my preparations for today's gathering with the neighbours. I leave out the bit about kissing Didier under the mistletoe last night, though: I'll fess up in due course, but right now it's a gift I want to treasure alone for a little while longer.

'I *am* good,' I say.

'Well, that's the best Christmas present I could possibly have.' I hear the smile in her voice. 'Oops, sorry Max, of course I mean the second-best present after yours! He's given me a new pair of walking boots. Which I thought wasn't exactly romantic, until he told me to look inside one of them and there was the booking confirmation for a holiday in the Italian Lakes in the spring. Quite imaginative, *n'est-ce pas?*'

'Full marks to Max. Give him my love, and to the boys too. See you soon. Merry Christmas to you all.'

I smile as I hang up, and then call my parents' number. Tess picks up, with a shriek of joy. 'It *is* her! Mom, Dad, it's Evie! Wait, I'm putting you on speakerphone...'

We exchange our news, our Christmas wishes, our love, the miles between us melting away like the thawing snow.

'I'm the size of a whale now; I'll email you a picture. And are you really coming back in February?'

'You betcha, Tess; wild horses wouldn't keep me away.'

'We can't wait to have you home, sweetie,' says my mother. 'And now the rest of you go start breakfast. I'm just going to have a word with Evie on my own. There, that's better, now I can hear myself think. I have some news for you. Good news, I think...'

Finally I hang up, sitting for a moment longer, gazing back down at the red-tiled roofs of Les Pélerins from which the last crusts of snow are now disappearing fast. And then I stride out, back down the hill to change out of my jeans and into something a little more suitable for Christmas entertaining, accompanied by the chuckle of the little stream which has thawed out now too and splashes along cheerily beside me.

◆ ◆ ◆

Didier arrives early—as I'd been hoping he would. He steps into the warm hallway and wraps his arms around me, immediately dispelling any possibility of awkwardness between us, confirming last night's kiss with another which, if anything, holds even more certainty: a promise of a future where love is more than just a possibility. We stay in each other's arms for a while, then he draws back and smiles. 'A Christmas gift for you,' he reaches into his coat pocket and brings out a half-bottle of golden wine. 'I'm sorry I wasn't able to get you something more à propos.'

'You just gave me the gift I was wishing for, Didier: that kiss. There's no need to give me anything more.' I scrutinise the label on the bottle and gasp. 'Château d'Yquem! The best sweet wine in the world. Don't tell me, another gift from a grateful patient?'

He nods. 'How did you guess? I thought it might be a suitable accompaniment to the famous Christmas pudding?'

'It'll be perfect. You surely do have friends in high places!'

He sniffs the air appreciatively as we go through to the kitchen to set out the aperitifs for Eliane and Mathieu's imminent arrival.

'Now,' I say, as I busy myself putting champagne flutes onto a tray. 'Before they come, I have a gift for you too. A while ago I emailed my mother about your anaesthesia machine. She has some contacts in the medical field in the States, through her fundraising work. So she spoke to someone who put her in touch with someone else... anyway, long story short, there's a guy who wants to talk to you. He's the CEO of a not-for-profit organisation which deals with healthcare in developing countries. They fund projects concerned with new medical technologies and they think your machine sounds really interesting. My mother says it's a shoe-in. I've got the guy's contact details. He wants you to call him as soon as possible after the holidays. They're really excited about the machine's capabilities and a possible tie-in with *Médecins Sans Frontières*. They're already talking in terms of you heading up the project, which would mean spending time in the States and in Africa too. Other countries in the future as well, if it goes to plan.'

Didier's very handsome jaw has, quite literally, dropped. He rakes his fingers through his hair—enhancing that Bradley Cooper look again—as he takes in what I'm saying.

'But how...? When...? What...?' And then, his eyes shining as realisation dawns, 'Why, Evie, it's a Christmas miracle! The best present you could possibly have given me. *Merci*, from the bottom of my heart.'

Just then there's a knock at the door and I leave him where he's sunk down onto a kitchen chair, still shaking his head in disbelief, to go let Eliane and Mathieu in.

In the sunny sitting room we open the bottle of champagne with a celebratory pop and raise our glasses to toast Christmas and friendship and other miracles, as Didier explains his machine—and the new possibilities for it now that there's a promise of funding—to our elderly neighbours.

As I pass round a plate of light-as-air cheese *gougères*, I can't help stealing frequent glances at his face, even more handsome when it's so animated, rejoicing that his dream is a step closer to becoming reality. I see Eliane notice, with her clear gaze, how often our eyes meet and then how he hugs me to him as he tells them about the funding, and I know she sees it all. I wonder what she sees in our futures... or maybe she saw it all last night and none of this comes as any surprise whatsoever. I'd love to know: is this the start of something lasting? Do the new paths that are opening up before us run alongside one another? Or will they take us off in different directions? I'm sure she knows. But I'm equally sure that, for Didier and for me, the adventure will be in finding out, taking our time, stepping out on these new paths and seeing where they lead. Letting

Fate do its thing, spreading our newly mended wings like fledglings as we learn to fly again.

I pass round the plate of aperitifs, urging Mathieu to take the last of the cheese puffs, and then go into the kitchen to heat the chestnut soup.

Suddenly, rudely interrupting the comfortable flow of chat next door as Mathieu and Eliane quiz Didier about his experiences in Africa, a strange noise drowns out the gentle bubbling of the pudding in its pan and the peaceful roar of the fire in the belly of the range. It's a loud and insistent beeping, underlain by a deep rumble that seems to make the very walls of the house shake. We crowd into the hallway. 'What on earth...?' I say, bewildered.

Flinging open the front door, we're confronted by the slowly reversing bulk of a vast truck that's edging into the yard, its tall sides catching the oaks' branches, causing the mistletoe to toss alarmingly, and sending a flurry of broken twigs cascading to the ground.

'The driver must be lost,' says Eliane, shaking her head disapprovingly. 'What *does* he think he's doing? He'll upset the horses.'

'On Christmas Day of all days too,' Didier exclaims.

The driver's door opens and a stout, balding man jumps down from the cab, giving us a cheery salute.

And then my jaw nearly hits the muddy ground. Because the passenger door opens and out clambers none other than that famous celebrity chef of the moment, my own estranged husband, Will Brooke.

'Thank goodness for satnav, hey, Dylan? We'd never have found this place without it. Surprise, Evie! Oh, and a very Merry Christmas to you all. Are we in time for lunch?'

For a few moments, all I can do is stand and gape. Is this another one of those dreams, where everything has been going so wonderfully and then suddenly, out of nowhere, Will turns up and throws cold water over it all, bringing me back to a reality that I'd really rather not confront? But no, Didier, Eliane and Mathieu are definitely real, standing there in the doorway behind me. And Will and the driver look pretty darn solid too.

My husband strides towards me across the yard, crunching through the crust of melting snow, and engulfs me in a warm bear hug. Out of the corner of my eye, I notice a slight flurry of movement as my three neighbours tactfully retreat into the house, giving us a moment. But what must Didier be thinking? And my own thoughts are a jumble of confusion as I struggle to make sense of what's happening here...

I draw back so I can see Will's beaming face. 'But what...? And how...?'

He laughs, delighted that the surprise has totally flummoxed me. 'Dylan, come and meet Evie.' He ushers the truck driver forward. 'Evie, this is Dylan Burke, trucker extraordinaire and knight in shining armour.'

I shake Dylan by the hand. 'Pleased to meet you,' I say, although I have to admit he makes a somewhat unlikely 'knight': with his cheerful, pudgy face and short stature he bears a more-than-passing resemblance to Danny DeVito.

'So this is the famous Evie,' he beams, pumping my hand up and down with enthusiasm. 'Will's told me all about you on the drive down.'

'Nightmare journey,' Will chips in. 'I got your email, Evie, and it made me realise how crazy this is, us being apart. So I jumped in the car as soon as I could get away. Managed to get as far as Orléans and then the snowstorm struck. The car's still stranded in a motorway service station. I had to sleep in it the night before last, bloody freezing it was. I kept turning the engine on so the heater would work, otherwise I might have died of hypothermia. Anyway, the next morning the whole place was completely snowed in, the car half-buried in a drift. Battery completely dead. I met Dylan here in the café. We waited until they'd ploughed the *autoroutes*—Dylan was listening in on the radio so he knew what was going on. Spent last night sleeping in the spare bunk in his cab. Then this morning he reckoned it was safe enough, so we set off again. What a hero; I wouldn't be here without you, mate.'

'It's no problem, Will, since I was coming this way in any case.' The cheery trucker turns to me. 'Got a delivery of wine to pick up and it turned out we were making for the same place. Reckoned seeing as I'd missed Christmas at home by now, I might as well carry on. Gotta get through, come hell or high water, that's my motto. Lucky your lane was so well gritted—wasn't sure we'd be able to get up it other-wise.'

'So here we are—just like the Three Wise Men, except there's only two of us. We made it just in time for Christmas, though I'd meant to get here a couple of days ago to surprise you.'

'Well, it certainly is a surprise!' I smile, a little wanly I guess, not entirely sure that I'm as pleased to see Will as he evidently is to see me. I pull myself together though. It *is* Christmas after all, and they have made a very impressive effort to get here through the snow. And what am I supposed to do, turn them away from the inn, behaving like The Grinch or Ebenezer Scrooge? Will and I clearly have some serious talking to do, but first of all, mindful of my guests, I figure we'd better have our Christmas lunch.

'Come in out of the cold. You're very welcome. And you got here just in time—we're about to sit down and eat.'

We crowd into the warm sitting room, where Didier pours the last of the champagne into two glasses for Will and Dylan, and I make the introductions. 'My neighbours, and very good friends, Eliane, Mathieu and Didier.' Will shakes their hands, still pleased with his surprise, sure of his welcome, secure in his right to be here. So I guess he's not picking up on the undercurrents of bewilderment (from Eliane and Mathieu), bemusement (from Didier), and awkward confusion (from me) that mingle with the scent of pine needles and wood smoke in the warm, sunlit room.

I hustle through to the kitchen to add two extra place settings to the table. Luckily there's easily enough food to go round as I've prepared enough to ensure I'd be eating leftovers (always the best bit of any Christmas meal) for several days to come. Didier comes into the room, carrying the empty champagne bottle.

'Didier, I'm sorry. I had no idea he was coming...'

He puts a finger on my lips, stopping me mid-sentence. 'It's okay, Evie.' He smiles, but there's a seriousness behind it. 'You don't have to explain. I think perhaps there is unfinished business between you and your husband?'

'Why, no! Well, not on my part anyway. I don't know...'

'Hush, Evie. Not now. I know this is difficult for you. If you want me to leave I will.'

I take his hands in mine for a moment. 'No, I don't want you to leave, Didier. That is the very last thing I want. I'm sorry; this isn't exactly how I'd planned the Christmas meal. And I don't know why Will's here, but it doesn't change anything...' I trail off, unconvincing and unconvinced.

Then Didier looks so sad, and he says, 'But yes, Evie. I think perhaps it changes everything.'

And I turn away because, in this moment, suddenly I don't know. Last night, I felt I'd woken up at last from a long sleep, my strength renewed, ready to contemplate a life filled with possibilities. But now, with the reality of Will's presence in the house, that future looks like a silly dream. How could I possibly have believed any of it could really come to pass in the cold light of day? I'm still married. I made those vows. I still owe it to Will to make another effort, especially in view of the effort he's made to get here, to be with me on Christmas Day. His atonement, perhaps, for not being there that other time when I needed him. Eliane said I have to forgive him. Does that mean getting back together, picking up where we left off? Reason—and the fact that I'm still legally married to him—says so. But, on the other hand, every instinct in my body is saying *non,* in a very French accent.

Pulling myself together, I serve the soup, lacing it with a swirl of cream. Will is regaling the assembled company with stories about filming his cookery programmes, switching effortlessly from English to fluent French for the benefit of Dylan, Eliane and Mathieu. I wonder, fleetingly, what's happened to his mystery assistant, Stephanie whatchamacallit, but I guess the answer is evident in Will's presence here.

'Mmm, this soup is delicious. What is it? Chestnut? What a great recipe! We'll have to incorporate it in a programme sometime.'

We? Is that the Royal We, Prince William? Or does he really mean 'we' as in Will-and-Evie? I glance across at Didier, but he's studiously avoiding catching my eye. The fact that he's concentrating hard on crumbling a piece of homemade soda bread into smaller and smaller pieces is the only clue as to what's going on in his head. Eliane looks at him and then at me, her wise grey eyes calmly taking it all in.

I turn to the truck driver, who's sitting beside me. 'So tell me, where are you from, Dylan?'

'Dudley. Centre of the universe. It's near Birmingham. I work for one of the biggest hauliers in England. "Logistics" as they call it nowadays.'

'And do you have family there?'

He nods, slurping his soup appreciatively. 'The missus and the two sprogs, Ziggy and Zowie.'

'Great names, aren't they?' Will chips in. 'As you can tell, Dylan's a huge Bowie fan.'

'Yeah. And my parents called me Dylan after Bob. They were big fans of his, y'see. So it's a bit of a tradition in my family. Rock 'n' roll!'

'But that's terrible that you've been separated from them at Christmas time,' Eliane exclaims when this is translated. 'They must be missing you very much, and you them.'

He nods. 'I wouldn't normally be on a long-haul trip at this time of the year. Make a point of being at home, usually. Only this year we were short-staffed. So I took this run, thinking I could do it there and back in two days, easy. That storm came out of nowhere, way worse than anything they were forecasting.'

'But you must call your family,' Eliane insists.

'I tried on the mobile just now, but can't get through.'

'Do you have Internet here, Evie?' asks Will. 'So he can call?'

I shake my head.

'I do,' offers Didier. 'After lunch you can come to my house and Skype them if you'd like. Fortunately everything came back on again this morning.'

'Oh, cheers mate, that'd be epic. I'm planning on kipping in the cab tonight—won't be going anywhere after this wine,' he holds his glass out so that Mathieu can re-fill it with some of the very good Bordeaux *rouge* from the château, 'but then I hope I can do the pick-up tomorrow morning and head home straight away. The rate this snow's melting, the roads should be clear by the morning.'

Didier gets up to help me clear the soup bowls. 'What else can I do, Evie?' he asks, as I smile my gratitude, eager to try and re-establish the connection between us that seems to be in danger of melting away, just as the snow's sparkle has melted from the apple tree beyond the window, leaving only bare, brown twigs once again. There's no sign of the robin, either, as if, with Will's arrival, the spell has been broken for him too.

'That's okay, thanks, Didier, I'll take it from here,' says Will, appearing between us, rolling up his sleeves and picking up the carving knife with a flourish. 'Here, Evie, I'll carve and you can serve. What is this? Pork loin stuffed with truffles? Wow, that's another *great* recipe.'

Didier retires gracefully, and as he goes back to his seat at the table, we exchange a glance. His expression is blank, giving nothing away as he takes in the cosy domestic scene with Will—playing a starring role as Master of the House—carving and me serving up the plates of food. All I need is a frilly apron and a starched cap and I'd be the archetypal French maid. I feel my hackles rising, but bite my tongue. This is hardly the time for a domestic disagreement, which could just open the long-closed floodgates of unfinished business between us. But I know how it must look to Didier, so I try to convey regret and the fact that Will's presence doesn't necessarily change things between us. Then I catch myself, realising that the word "necessarily" is the key one here. Of course, as Didier said, Will's presence changes everything. I *am* officially still married to him, after all. And—a ghastly thought suddenly occurs to me—perhaps Didier thinks I've been playing him along, deceiving him as to exactly how separated Will and I actually are. Will isn't helping this possible scenario either. He's breezed in here, acting as if it's his undisputed right to march in and take over. Too much exposure to celebrity will do that, I guess. His ego has clearly grown somewhat in the past year and now he's beginning to believe his own publicity, seeing himself as the star of the show wherever he goes. Well, he always did enjoy an audience...

We settle back down at the table and raise our glasses of 2009 Bordeaux Supérieur (an excellent year, Mathieu pronounces, with an appreciative smack of his lips).

'To the chef,' Didier says, his eyes meeting mine.

'Thank you, everyone,' butts in Will, taking the credit for having carved the pork. 'And to Evie too,' he adds, magnanimously. 'Great meal, babe.'

It's such a barefaced cheek that I have to stop myself from gasping in annoyance by taking a sip of my wine.

I raise my glass towards Will and Dylan. 'And to unexpected guests.' I emphasise the word "unexpected" just a tad. 'It's such a surprise having you here, Dylan, Will.'

Will nods, choosing to ignore the fact that I've put a little distance between us for Didier's benefit.

'Yeah, I know. It's been so hectic with all the publicity and the interviews, and I'm going straight back into the studio in January to film a new series. But when I got your email, Evie, I realised what's really important is us. Time we got back on track, eh, now you're your old self again. I said to the production team I want you on the show. Non-negotiable. Of course, they want me to carry on fronting it, because—as they say—I *am* the show. But there's a role for you, Evie. And I reckon we can take it even further, working together as a team.'

Rose's prediction, all those weeks ago, comes back to haunt me: *'I give him a year. He'll soon realise how much he needs you and your recipes once the honeymoon period wears off.'*

Despite the fact that it's Christmas and I'm the hostess here—and I ought, therefore, to remain gracious and serene at all times—my temper flares. Well, I'm not a French-Irish redhead for nothing.

'We'll have to see, Will. We have a lot of talking to do.' I fix him with a steely glare. 'Things have changed in the past year, for me as well as for you. I'm not so sure I'll ever be my "old self" again. And maybe that's a good thing.'

Didier looks up suddenly, from where he's been concentrating hard on chasing a morsel of meat around his plate. And do I imagine it, or is there a gleam of fresh hope in his eyes?

Will's expression of bewilderment at my outburst morphs suddenly into one of suspicion as he intercepts this glance.

'But for the moment,' I continue, regaining my composure, 'let's just enjoy our Christmas meal and be thankful that we have so much when there are others who have so little.'

Eliane, who's been watching these exchanges closely, her expression one of calm amusement, picks up on the cue and helps me out. She turns to Didier. 'Tell us, have you had news from Africa? What's happening in South Sudan now? We seem to hear so little in the news these days. Is it still as troubled there...?'

Will looks a little petulant as the conversation is diverted from him, but he quickly perks up again as he engages Dylan in a conversation about the new TV series.

'Can't wait to get home and tell them that I had that Will Brooke in my cab,' the trucker chuckles.

'I'll get you and your wife tickets for the show if you'd like,' Will offers magnanimously, back in celeb mode again.

'Could you, mate? That'd be epic. She's your biggest fan!'

Didier helps clear the plates, and I smile my gratitude to him.

'And now, against all the odds, the Christmas pudding!' I turn it out carefully onto a serving plate and begin to warm a little Cognac gently in a pan. 'The Château d'Yquem is in the fridge. Would you like to open it, Didier?'

Will materialises once again, insinuating himself between us, and now I'm definitely getting the impression that this is turning into a testosterone-fuelled contest.

I smile, ruefully. I guess I should be pleased to have Prince William and Bradley Cooper slugging it out over me—insofar as their impeccable English manners and French *courtoisie* allow them to slug, that is—but my potential enjoyment of the situation is ruined by the fact that I know I'm going to end up hurting one of them. For all his bravado, Will has shared some of the darkest, deepest moments of my pain, and I can see that, without the timely distraction of his new-found television career, he would have been a broken man. Fleetingly I wonder again, should I give our marriage another chance? It's certainly true that I've changed during my time here, managing, at last, to find a way to live again after losing Lucie. But do I want to go back to life in London? To the glamour and reflected glory of being Will's wife? To start over? Try for another baby who will help heal our loss? It's a safer option than the alternative: launching out on my own; going back to the States to try and find a publisher for my book; maybe opening a bistro of my own somewhere; or perhaps fulfilling the Thibaults' vision of a cookery school in a French château, bringing the world to this beautiful corner of France. And then, out there too, there's the possibility of a relationship with Didier. Is our connection as profound for him as it is for me? Are we too damaged, in our different ways, to be able to embark on learning to love again, or does our pain bind us together in an understanding that goes deeper than anything I've ever known before with another man?

I ponder these questions as I stand at the range, breathing in the rich fumes that the warm Cognac is beginning to exude. And perhaps their heady potency acts like smelling salts, because suddenly the confusion in my head clears and I see a scene from my childhood so vividly that it's as if it's a signpost that points the way forward with absolute certainty.

I remember standing at the top of a snow-covered hill, the rope of my sled in my be-mittened hand, and Tess standing next to me. We're wearing bobble hats that *Mamie* Lucie has knitted for us for Christmas, mine blue, Tess's red. And we have a choice before us: to take the more gentle route down the slope, where others have gone before, which, I know, will result in a safe and graceful glide to the bottom of the hill where our parents await us. Or I can carve out my own route, risking the steeper side of the hill where no one else has dared to venture yet. I know the ride there won't be smooth; it may involve a few bumps, some unseen moguls, a spill or two. I'll need to use all my strength and skill to steer a safe course through the hazardous dark patch of pine trees at the start of the run. But the rewards will be far greater. I'll fly across the virgin snow with breathtaking speed, the sunlight that reflects off the perfect white surface and the pure, cold air making my cheeks glow and my spirits soar. I'll depend on my own wits, my own sense of self-belief, to navigate a route of my own making. And if I fall, or if the sled turns over, I'll pick myself up and start again. Because when I arrive at my destination, it will all have been worth it, and the hugs and laughter of my parents will be all the sweeter. I look at Tess and I nod, suddenly certain. 'You can follow me if you want,' I say. And the doubt in her face clears, because she believes in me and she knows that, together, we can do this. And, all of a sudden, having a sister is the very best feeling in the world.

Afterwards, when we finally land in a laughing heap, just a little battered and bruised from our precipitous descent, our mom and dad pick us up and dust the powdery snow off our clothes, and my mother says, 'That's my girls. Beautiful and bold!' I can hear her voice, as clearly as if she's standing here beside me now.

I look across to where Didier and Will are engaged in a polite tussle over who's going to open the precious bottle of Château d'Yquem. 'Will, could you fetch the smaller wine glasses from that cabinet, please?' I firmly hand Didier the corkscrew. 'And now I'm ready to light the pudding. So if you wouldn't mind taking your seats...'

The rich, dark sides of the Christmas pudding shine as I pour the warmed Cognac over them and hold a lit match a little way off so the alcohol fumes catch. A beautiful blue flame flickers, as ethereal as St Elmo's fire, as I carry the dish to the table to a round of applause from Eliane, Mathieu and Dylan.

Didier pours a little of the honey-gold wine into our glasses to savour before we embark on the pudding, so that we can enjoy the full effect of the sweetly nuanced nectar before allowing its complex fullness to mingle with the dessert on our taste buds. The wine is gorgeous and its soft, rounded sweetness makes me think of sun-ripe apricots, and honey collected drop by precious drop by industrious bees from the throats of summer flowers. As the light outside begins to fade on this all-too-short winter's day, Didier's wine helps to remind us of the promise of long summer's evenings still to come, spent lingering on a terrace at the end of a perfect day, the warmth of the air caressing sun-kissed skin...

But just now, for today, we'll make do with a glass of distilled sunshine, shared in unexpected company, and we'll offer up a little 'thank you' for it all, in the spirit of Christmas.

After our meal, as dusk falls and the first lights begin to come on, one by one, in the valley below, Didier pushes back his chair. 'I hate to break up the party, but I'm sure, Dylan, that you are eager to speak to your family. Evie, this was a magnificent meal. A most memorable one, too.'

I move across to him, and Will's head swivels to watch us as I take both Didier's hands in mine. 'Thank you, Didier. For the delicious wine, and for so much more besides.'

'This has been a happy Christmas for you after all, I think,' he says. 'And for that I am very pleased.' His smile belies the pain and doubt that I can see have crept back in, just visible in the fine lines around his eyes.

'I hope it's been happy for you too. I'll see you tomorrow.' It's a statement, not a question; a coded reassurance.

He nods, accepting that Will and I have to talk and so, right now, there are no promises. But there is still hope.

I help Eliane on with her coat and she hugs me. '*Merci*, Evie, for good food and friendship. And remember, what I said last night: that whatever we humans do to complicate things, Fate has a way of making everything work out as it's meant to be in the end. It's really very simple.'

I step out into the dusk to say goodbye to her and Mathieu, glancing across to where Didier has ushered Dylan into his house and is just closing the door. He raises his hand in a final, grave salute. I realise that Will has materialised behind me and he drapes an arm across my shoulders proprietarily, playing his role as the master of the house again as he waves goodbye to his guests.

Lucie's candle burns steadily in the window, the flame unwavering. Suddenly, out from the gloom within the barn, a large white shape swoops, flying so low over our heads that we involuntarily duck. 'Wow! Did you see that?' Will exclaims. 'What was it? It flew so low I could even hear the wind beneath its wings!'

I can't help but laugh.

'What?' he says.

'Nothing. Just something Rose once said to me along those very lines. A timely reminder.' I watch as the ghostly shape disappears, soaring off into the night, having delivered its message from the spirit world loud and clear.

We step back into the warmth of the house, and Will and I are finally alone. We stand in the hallway for an awkward moment and then he makes a move towards me, a little tentative, less sure of himself without his audience. I stand there, moving neither forwards nor back and I look him square in the eye. 'Will, it's wonderful to have you here on Christmas Day, and I am totally awe-struck at the effort you've made to get here through the snow. But I'm sorry; I can't go back to what we had.'

He starts to object, but I take him by the hand and lead him through to the sitting room, gesturing him to sit down on the sofa beside me.

'We've been through so much together, Will, and we haven't always been able to support each other in the ways that we should have done, perhaps, but it's time to put it all behind us now. We both need to move on and I need to follow your example and start living again.' He begins to interject, but I hold up a hand to stop him. 'And I'm afraid that means separately. I have to follow my own path now. My future doesn't lie in London, and it doesn't lie with you.'

He gazes into the embers of the fire that glow deep red as they die away, and I see the unshed tears which gleam softly in his eyes. I lay a hand on top of his.

'I know. It's sad. But we were too young, our marriage too green, to be able to survive losing Lucie. If we tried to carry on, tried to make a life together again, it would stop both of us from becoming the people we really can be. Coming away has given me that perspective, helped me to see things more clearly. You know how it goes in our world: there can only ever be one chef in charge of the kitchen. I wish you well with your career: I know it's going to be a glittering one, and I want you to enjoy it to the full. And I hope there'll be someone out there to enjoy it with you; you deserve much love and much happiness.'

'I'd hoped it would be you, Evie,' he says softly. 'I hoped I could make up for not being there when you needed me most, that I could be the one to make it better. That's why I took the job, because I thought maybe if I did I could show you the way out of your sorrow; I just needed to lead the way.'

I nod, understanding now. And forgiveness—true forgiveness—washes over me like a wave. And as it recedes, I find my anger has gone, washed away, just like that, leaving behind a feeling of complete peace, complete clarity. 'Oh, Will, you always were my guide. You led me along paths I might never have taken otherwise. Were it not for you, I never would have gone to London, and I might never have found out how much I loved running the bistro. You led the way for me. But I need to take another path now, carve out my own way down the mountain.'

I know there'll be spills *en route*, but I know, too, that I will grow along the way as I rely on my instincts and my own intuition, making my way along my own pilgrim path. And when I arrive at the bottom, the sense of exhilaration will make the trials and tribulations all worthwhile.

We sit, side by side, in silence for a long while. And then Will turns to me with a smile. 'Friends?' he asks.

'Of course,' I smile. 'I'll be following your career with interest. I'll be proud that I know the famous and talented Will Brooke.' We embrace and it feels okay to draw away again afterwards. It feels right.

There's a tap at the door and Dylan pushes it open. 'It's only me,' he calls. 'Spoke to the wife and kids. All's well in Dudley.'

'Good,' says Will, and he smiles at me. 'And now, Evie, can you show us where the things are to make up a couple of beds? No offence, Dylan, but it'll be nice not to have to sleep in the cab of your truck tonight.'

The trucker looks from Will to me and back again, considering what this must mean, and then nods. 'No worries, mate, no offence taken. And then we'll get started on the washing up. That was a cracking meal, Evie. Even beats turkey and all the trimmings. I've told the missus that I'll see if I can contact the château owners first thing in the morning, go and pick up the consignment. That way I can be back home late tomorrow night. I can give you a lift back to the service station if you want it, Will, so you can pick up your car.'

'Cheers, Dylan. That would work well. I'll need to be getting back. Got a few things to sort out before I'm due back in the studio again...'

♦ ♦ ♦

Next morning, the winter sun is just beginning to edge itself above the horizon, flushing the sky the colour of a robin's rosy breast, as the three of us stand in the yard saying our farewells. Dylan clambers into his cab and turns the key in the ignition, eager to be on the road again, but giving Will and me a moment alone under the covering thrum of the motor.

Will enfolds me in his arms and I hug him back, a little pang of loss and regret binding us together in one final embrace. We stand like that for a minute, saying nothing because there's nothing more to be said. He draws back finally and smiles down at me. 'I wish it had been different, Evie. But I'm glad we can part as friends. I'll be in touch about finalising the divorce. I was thinking about it last night, and I'm going to sign the London house over to you in its entirety.' I start to protest, but he holds up a hand to stop me. 'No, let me do that. I'm happy in my new apartment. You can choose what to do with the house; keep it as an investment or sell it. The money might come in handy if you're thinking of starting up a new bistro in Boston. Or if you need something to live off while you're writing your cookbook. I'm looking forward to giving it a plug on my show, by the way.'

There's a movement behind one of the windows in Didier's house, a shadow that blocks the light there for a moment and then moves away again.

Will notices me notice it. 'I suppose you might be needing a few plane tickets between Boston and France as well.' He smiles again, just a little ruefully, giving me his blessing.

'Thank you,' I whisper. 'I wish it had been different too, Will.'

He climbs into the passenger side of the cab and pulls the heavy door closed after him, lowering the window to lean out and wave, as Dylan lets the brakes off with a hiss and a sigh and the wheels begin to roll, edging the bulk of the trailer back out onto the lane.

As I watch the tail lights wink red and then disappear down the road, the chill bite of the winter wind seems to ease a little and the sun hauls itself up a little higher, into the branches of the oak tree beside me. A flutter of wings catches my eye as the robin swoops down from one of the twigs to peck at the soft ground where the snow has melted.

'Well, hello there,' I smile. 'Good to have you back!'

And do I imagine it, or is the breeze that strokes my cheek a little warmer suddenly?

I know, now, that our lives are made up of changing seasons. Through the darkest days of bleak midwinter we have to do what we can to keep the faith, nourishing our bodies and our souls, keeping a flame burning—no matter how tiny or how tenuous—deep down inside our hearts. And that, in the bleakest moments of all, we should make a Christmas for ourselves, piling on the tinsel, lighting the candles and the fairy lights and rolling back the darkness that threatens to encroach, with the promise of a rebirth; a reawakening; a *Réveillon*. Because, if we can just hang on in there long enough, spring will return and the leaves, hidden deep within the bare branches and the stark vine stocks, will unfurl to the sunlight with tender, new promise.

As I watch the robin hop and bob amongst the last vestiges of melting snow that lie at my feet, a spike of bright green catches my eye. It's the first spring bulb, pushing its way defiantly upwards towards the blue winter sky, a sky which soars above me, drawing my spirits to soar there with the birds. On my own widespread wings.

And you know, I think Eliane's ability to see the future must be catching. Because suddenly, clear as the morning light, I have a vision of a little bistro on a Boston street corner, its name picked out in antique gold lettering: *Chez Lucie*. There will be a candle burning in the window and fresh flowers on the tables, and the air will smell of newly baked soda bread. And copies of my cookbook will be for sale on the counter. I can see it so clearly that I can even read the title: *Mamie Lucie's Kitchen*. The old and the new in perfect harmony. My roots and my wings.

That shadow passes across the window in Didier's house again. I hesitate for a moment, considering. I know I don't *need* anyone else; I can steer my own path down the mountain, counting on my own skill and strength to negotiate my way through the trees and the moguls and the icy patches.

But needing and *wanting* are two different things.

I stand on tiptoe and break off a sprig of the mistletoe that hangs just above my head. Crossing the yard, I knock on Didier's door.

He opens it straight away, a smile as warm as spring sunshine lighting up his face, his expression as full of promise and hope as my future suddenly seems.

I hold the green sprig above my copper curls.

'If it's not too late, Merry Christmas, Didier.'

He pulls me to him and wraps me in his arms.

'It's never too late, Evie,' he smiles. 'Merry Christmas.'

Epilogue:
Nearly two years later...

As I step out of the plane it's like opening an oven door: the smell of Africa engulfs me, tantalisingly exotic. It's the scent of heat and dust, with undercurrents of something dark and wild, something untameable. The tarmac bounces the sun's brutal rays back up at me and I follow the line of passengers wading through the thick air which shimmers with oily heat. A few small, white clouds are suspended in the vast, overarching sky, wider than any sky I've ever stood beneath before. As we wait outside the door of the terminal—although it's more of a shed really—I watch the sun-bleached grass that lines the runway shimmer and shift in the haze of hot air, oil fumes and dust. I blink in the strong sunshine, fumbling in my purse for my sunglasses, my eyes unaccustomed to so much light and colour having come straight from a Massachusetts winter.

At last a key is located, the door unlocked, and we shuffle through the baggage reclaim and then emerge through the frosted glass door, beyond which the world's newest country awaits.

My heart leaps as I spot his face in the crowd and he pushes forwards through the jostling throng to claim me before the taxi touts and hotel hustlers can. He folds me in his arms and I breathe in the smell of his skin, familiar and reassuring beneath the atmosphere of sweat and rotting garbage and car fumes that engulfs us. He takes my bag and we walk, hand in hand, to his rental jeep in the car park. We can't stop looking at each other, grinning at each other, unable to believe we're both really here.

'How is everyone?' he asks. 'I never thought you'd be able to tear yourself away from the bistro to get here.'

I laugh. 'I know; it wasn't easy. But it's in safe hands. Hélène's taken to it like a duck to water; she's a natural-born manager. I guess all her experience with organising weddings has really paid off. And Tess will look in at lunchtimes and lend a hand if it's needed. But I trust the team completely. I know they'll be fine. Anyway, it's good practice for all of us. I'll be running the first courses at Château Bellevue in two months' time, so I need to be able to leave them to it sometimes. But now tell me everything. How's the roll-out of the machines going?'

Didier laughs, running his fingers through his dark hair and raising his shoulders in a very French shrug. 'It's Africa, Evie, so of course there've been frustrating hold-ups along the way, but it's going well. We've got the machines in three of the biggest hospitals now and we're making progress in the clinics in the refugee camps in Jonglei province. I can't wait to show you. And tomorrow you'll see the feeding station for the children in the Juba camp. Everyone's so excited to meet you. The children have been learning a special song for the official opening. One of them asked me if you're the queen of America! I showed them your photo, and one of the bistro back in Boston so they'd be able to picture where the funding for the feeding station is coming from. They thought you looked like a queen because, they said, your hair is like a shining crown.'

We pull up in front of the hotel where we'll be staying tonight before heading out to the camp tomorrow.

'They all wanted me to bring you straight there, but I thought you'd be tired after all that travelling.

And anyway, I want you to myself for one night at least, before you are claimed by two hundred children and their mothers...'

◆ ◆ ◆

I have hundreds of photos from that week in South Sudan, taken to show the folks back home who have given their time and their money and their love to bring a little extra joy to children who need it. The *Chez Lucie* feeding station will help ensure some hungry bellies are filled, some babies given the nourishment they need, which can be so hard to come by in this troubled, turbulent land. Some of my favourite pictures are of the smiles, those eyes that have seen so much fear and pain shining, for this moment at least, with the light of pure joy.

But my very favourite moment of all wasn't captured on camera.

I was holding a tiny baby girl in the camp, cradling her in my arms as she guzzled hungrily from her bottle, when Didier came into the tent. He hunkered down in front of us, watching my face, and I raised my eyes to his. 'Just getting in a little practice,' I said to him, keeping my expression serious, being careful not to give away the happiness that was bubbling through my veins and threatening to overflow, at any moment, in a messy combination of laughter and tears. 'Because,' I went on, 'I guess in, oh, about seven months' time, I'm going to be needing it.'

There was a moment's pause as I looked back down at the perfect curve of the infant's cheek, brushed by her lashes as, sated finally, her eyes began to close.

And then Didier put a hand on my arm. 'Evie, do you mean...?' He couldn't finish the sentence for the big lump of hope that had lodged itself in his throat. And then his eyes lit up, realisation dawning like a sunrise in winter.

He looked searchingly into my face. 'But how are you feeling? Have you been okay?'

'I'm good. A little tired, but the nausea hasn't been nearly as bad this time. The doctor says she's going to keep a close watch on things, but everything's looking fine; I should be okay to travel for a few months more.'

Then he gathered me into his arms. And as we held each other tight, I whispered, so as not to wake the baby sleeping in my arms, 'Let's tell everyone on Christmas Eve, once your parents have arrived in Boston. When we're all there. The whole family, together...'

Letter from Fiona

Thank you so much for reading *The French for Christmas*. I hope that Evie's journey has entertained, moved and inspired you. If you, or someone close to you, has been affected by stillbirth or miscarriage, there is a further message for you following this letter.

Christmas is a time for giving and, in buying this book, you have helped make a difference. I have pledged to donate 10% of any royalties I receive from sales of *The French for Christmas* to the charity *Médecins Sans Frontières* (*Doctors Without Borders*) in support of their work all over the world, providing care and medical aid where it's needed most. Please visit my website—fionavalpy.com—for more details and updates. And you can find out more about Médecins Sans Frontières at www.msf.org

If you enjoyed this book, I'd be so grateful if you'd write a review. I love getting feedback and your review can help other readers find my books.

Finally, if you'd like to receive and email when my next book is released, you can **sign up to my mailing list at:**

Fionavalpy.com/Fiona-valpy-email-sign-up

I'll only send emails when I have a new book to share and I won't share your email address with anyone else.

With thanks and best wishes,
Fiona

PS. If you enjoyed The French for Christmas, I'm sure you'd love my other books – *The French for Love* and *The French for Always.*

Stillbirth:

sources of support

Whilst the vast majority of pregnancies in developed countries end in the safe and joyful arrival of a healthy baby, stillbirth is the sad outcome in a small proportion of cases. If this has happened to you, or to someone close to you, then I'm so sorry: you have my deepest sympathy and I send you a hug of condolence. I hope you have the loving support of friends and family to help you and that you can find the time and space you need to grieve. And I hope too that, like Evie, when the time is right you will find the strength and the courage to live your life with joy, on behalf of the child you've lost.

More support, advice and information, as well as lists of other organisations that can offer support, are available here:

In the UK: www.uk-sands.org (Stillbirth and Neo-natal Death Charity)

In the USA: www.firstcandle.org (offers a free brochure, *Surviving Stillbirth*)

THE FRENCH FOR LOVE

Can happy-ever-after get lost in translation?

Gina has lost her perfect job, her boyfriend and her favourite aunt all within the space of a few months. So when she inherits her aunt's ramshackle French house, Gina decides to pack her bags for the Bordeaux countryside – swapping English weather for blue skies, sunshine, great wine and a fresh start.

What she hasn't factored in is a hole in the roof, the *most* embarrassing language faux pas, and discovering family secrets that she was never supposed to know.

Suddenly feeling a long way from home, Gina will have to rely on new found friends, her own hard work – and Cédric – her charming, mysterious and *très* handsome new stonemason.

But whilst desire needs no translation, love is a different matter. Can Gina overcome the language barrier to make her French dream come true?

***The French for Love* is available now.**

THE FRENCH FOR ALWAYS

Five weddings. The perfect venue. One little hitch...

Leaving the grey skies of home behind to transform a crumbling French Château into a boutique wedding venue is a huge leap of faith for Sara. She and fiancé Gavin sink their life savings into the beautiful Château Bellevue – set under blue skies and surrounded by vineyards in the heart of Bordeaux.

After months of hard work, the dream starts to become a reality – until Gavin walks out halfway through their first season. Overnight, Sara is left very much alone with the prospect of losing everything.

With her own heart breaking, Sara has five weddings before the end of the season to turn the business around and rescue her dreams. With the help of the locals and a little French *courage*, can she save Château Bellevue before the summer is over?

The French for Always is available now.

33751982R00151

Printed in Great Britain
by Amazon